BLURRED LINES

TARRAH ANDERS

To my husband, who found his soulmate.
(Yeah, that's me!)

To my husband, who found his soulmate.
(Yeah, that's me!)

ONE

"ARE YOU FUCKING SERIOUS?" I feel like my eyes will burn from the sight. "I can't even right now!" I say with disdain as I slam the door to the bedroom.

I spin on my heel, my body rigid and my blood boiling from what I just saw in the room. The sound of my heels on the tile floor is all I hear as I dash to the kitchen counter for my purse.

Fuck this. I don't need to be treated like a piece of shit from someone who isn't worthy of my time. I walk over to the hall closet and grab one of the spare duffel bags on the top of the shelf and slam the door.

I walk around the living room and grab what is mine and cramming it in the bag as the bedroom door flies open.

"Sum! Sum!" Colin calls out while walking down the short hallway of the apartment that we both share. He sees me across the room and starts in my direction. "It's not what it looks like," he pleads.

"Are you kidding? Your dick in someone else is," I laugh,

"not what it looks like? You are fucking extra. You're a scumbag Colin, a fucking scumbag, and I'm done." I turn around and make my way to the other part of the living room, pulling some books off the bookshelf.

"What are you doing?" He asks.

"I'm getting some of my shit, I can't believe I thought that you were better than that."

"Listen," he starts.

"No, you listen. That bitch is still in the bedroom, the bedroom that you and I have shared for the past six months. You don't get to ask me to listen to you. I'm done. I'll be back later to grab the rest of my stuff. This relationship is so fucking over." I move around him and grab my purse with its contents falling over the hardwood floor.

Colin comes to my side, hands me things that I swiftly pull from his hands and stuff back into my purse. I say nothing to him as I finish adding my belongings back to the safety of my purse.

"I don't know why you have so much crap in that thing," he shakes his head standing.

"It's none of your fucking business," I sneer at him as the bedroom door opens.

"Colin?" Her tiny voice calls out while her small body fills the space of the doorway.

"Your slut is calling, Colin, you better go to her."

"Summer, c'mon, can we just talk about this?"

"There's nothing to say, I'll return my keys to the property manager as soon as my stuff is out of here." I walk to the front door, turn around for one last look of the apartment that I loved that is now tarnished, and exit.

I'm sitting in the driver's seat of my car before the tears begin to fall.

Why do I always date the jerks?

I've been dating Colin for a year and we've been living together for the past six months. I met him in a bar and ignored the things that people would say about his promiscuous ways and how he's never really been in a committed relationship, but I thought that he and I together were different.

I knew, deep down, that Colin was never the guy that I was going to marry. Hell, I'm not even sure that I want to get married. Ever.

Going at the rate that I am at thirty, it could very well be non existent for my future.

I hit the steering wheel and take a deep breath.

One. Two. Three.

I pull out my phone and call my girlfriend, Sloane.

"Sloane here," she answers.

"I need you," I say immediately.

"Are you okay?" She asks with concern in her tone.

"Colin and I are over, and I need you plus drinks and maybe a bit of ice cream, who am I kidding, I need a lot of ice cream, gallons and shit."

"Shit sweetie, I really wish I could right now, but I've got back-to-back parent-teacher meetings for the next three hours. I think Shaw just left for the day. Want to call him and see if he can watch you until I'm done?"

"I'm not a child, I don't need a babysitter," I reply dryly.

"I know, I'm just saying, so someone is with you in your time of need," she explains.

"Oh, maybe. Shaw hated Colin, so I'm not sure he'd be much support, but you're right. Plus, I can't just sit in the parking lot, drinks when you're done?"

"I'll be drink ready around six. I'm sorry love, I can't cancel these, the usual spot?"

"Yeah, the usual spot, see you there."

I hang up with her and inhale a deep breath again. I look up at the apartment building.

Moving to this building was my decision. I wanted this specific apartment, Colin was fine with whatever I chose, in fact he left most of the process to me, which looking back at it now, should have been a sign that he wasn't really invested, right?

Shaw is my other best friend and even though I call him first for most things, he hated Colin. I don't want to hear the 'I told you so,' but then again, I don't want to sit here in this parking lot a minute later.

I start the car and wait for the Bluetooth button to show on my car stereo screen and push the prompts until the call is connected. I put the car in reverse and start making my way to Shaw's house.

"You home yet?" I ask him.

"I'm getting Mason, and then I'll be home. Why? What's going on?"

"Can I come over for a bit? I'll tell you when you get home?"

"Sure, I should be there in twenty, let yourself in." He tells me.

Five minutes later, I'm pulling into Shaw's driveway, before shutting off the engine. My phone rings over the speakers and I see Colin's name. I reject the call, shut off the car and get out.

As I'm walking up the walkway to the porch, my phone rings from inside my purse. I don't bother with it and use my key to Shaw's house to open the door.

I set my purse on the chair in the living room and head straight to the fridge.

Shaw has a kid, so he's got to have some junk food in the house that I can get into to satisfy the sugar part of this break-up. I find some Go-Gurts and grab the whole box and sit at the kitchen table. I'm on my third when I hear the front door slam, multiple pairs of shoes slap against the floor as the sound rounds into the dining room.

"Auntie Summer!" Mason yells when he sees me. He jumps onto my lap, throws his tiny arms around my neck and hugs me tight. I return his hug as this is just what I needed and smile.

"Hey bud," I say into his short blond hair as Shaw pulls out a chair from the table and sits opposite me.

"Why are you eating all my gurts?" He points to the mess in front of me and then swings his head to look at Shaw. "Daddy, we're gonna need some more of these, start!"

"Start?" Shaw questions.

"Like right away," Mason clarifies.

"Oh, that would be STAT. I'll get some later. Go put your stuff away in your room while I talk to Summer," he directs.

Mason climbs off my lap and does as requested while Shaw looks me over.

"Do we need something more adult than yogurt?" He asks.

"I do, but I'm saving that for the bar," I reply. "If I start drinking, then I'm not leaving."

"Shit, what happened, did you get fired?" He asks.

"I own the store; I cannot really fire myself. No, it's about Colin." I say carefully.

"What did that idiot do now?"

TWO

I OPEN another of Mason's yogurts and begin squirting it into my mouth while Shaw looks on.

"He is fucking someone else," I say with a mouthful.

"Excuse me?" Shaw says, his tone bordering pissed off and concern.

"I left the store early today, I had Becky and Tasha there, so I thought it would be great to go home and make a nice dinner to surprise Colin for tonight, only to find that he was already home."

"Okay," Shaw says slowly.

"I got home, noticed a jacket that wasn't mine on the couch, and then I heard something from the bedroom. The door was closed, and you know since I live there, I didn't knock. So, when I opened up the door, there was Colin on the bed with some chick riding him. Neither of them noticed me right away and then when Colin did, she kept going and I just slammed the door closed."

"Shit, are you all right?" He asks.

"I started putting random shit in a bag and then I just left. I'm not going to kick him out. Who knows how many surfaces of that apartment are tainted, and now I don't have a home. I have no home, Shaw!" I begin to feel the tears surfacing.

"Confession time," Shaw begins with one of our truth bomb moments that we started back in college when we needed to be real with one another. "I never liked Colin, you were too good for him and he was a complete douche-canoe."

Shaw was out of his seat in a flash and to my side on his knees. His arms wrap around me and I lean into him, with tears falling.

"Daddy, why is Auntie Summer sad?" Mason asks from the front of the dining room.

"Hey bud, can you go play for a little bit? I need to make sure that Auntie Summer is okay."

I assume that Mason has left the room, as both of Shaw's arms are wrapped around me again.

"You've always got a home here, you know that. I have an extra room that you can stay in for as long as you need."

"I don't want to bring my drama into your house," I cry into his shoulder.

"Sum, you did that the moment you crashed my study group, go hang out with Mason for a little bit, I'll make sure the bed is made up for you and seriously, just stay here as long as you need."

"Are you sure?" I ask, pulling back and lifting my chin to look up at him with a sniff.

"Positive." He looks down and smiles sincerely.

"Thank you, Shaw. I promise to not suck as a temporary roommate."

"At least be cleaner than a four-year-old." He says with a tilt of his head.

"Deal."

"WAIT A MINUTE! You actually walked in on it?" Sloane asks, putting down her drink.

I just relayed everything that happened earlier tonight, and I feel like I need to rub my entire body with hand sanitizer.

"It was as if she was singing that 'Ride a horse' song." I reply.

"You mean 'Save a horse, ride a cowboy'." Sloane corrects with a laugh.

"Yeah, that. Anyway, she didn't notice me because she was likely reciting the lyrics, only thing missing was her arm up in the air!"

"Was she cute?" Sloane asks.

"I didn't get a look at her face, and it happened so quick."

"Do you think that it was a one time thing?" Sloane asks.

"I don't know, I don't care. I won't be with someone who cheats on me."

"Smart woman. So now what, I want to say that you guys just moved in together?"

"Six months ago. Shaw has an extra room, so I'll just stay there until I can find something else." I shrug.

"Is Shaw dating anyone?" she asks.

"Not that I know of, why?" I ask, running my thumb along the condensation of my glass.

"Shaw's cute," she's with a lift of her shoulder in a nonchalant tone.

"I guess so, why do you say that?"

"Have you ever, you know?" she wiggles her eyebrows.

"Have I what?" I look at her in confusion.

"Gone there... you know, with Shaw?"

I laugh. She can't be serious.

"Um, no. Shaw and I are just friends. He's my best friend, we've never, you know." I say between laughing.

"Really? Shaw's hot. If I didn't have Roger, I would be all over that. He's got that hot dad look to him, he may not have a six-pack or anything, but damn–have you seen his face?" She fans herself.

"Really? Shaw?"

"You may have the friend's lens on and all, but he's a hot commodity. I've heard some of the mom's talk about him from time to time after leaving his classroom."

"He's Shaw, I've never thought of him like that." I shake my head.

"Maybe you should start? It couldn't hurt. He'd be good for you."

"I don't need to jump into another relationship, so quickly. Let alone with my best friend."

"Try looking at him differently, just try."

I spin in my seat to face forward to order another round of drinks.

Shaw. I don't think I've ever noticed Shaw in any other light before, could I?

THREE

Summer

I'M HUNGOVER.

It sucks, because it's been awhile since I've felt this shitty and I was also hoping that the past 24 hours would have been forgotten. Instead, they are crisp in my memory, including what Sloane mentioned about Shaw.

I met Shaw my sophomore year in college when I arrived an hour late to an English Lit study group When everyone else was annoyed by my tardiness, he took the time to catch me up.

I ran late to the next one as well, and again, he caught me up. We forged a friendship and only grew closer in the later years after college.

Looks-wise, Shaw is an attractive man. He's tall, light brown hair that's a little long on top and short on the sides, he's got caring olive colored eyes and a strong jawline.

Am I attracted to him? I don't think that I ever let myself think of him as anything more than a friend. When we first met, I was dating some frat guy, and he was focused on school and dated here and there, but nothing too serious until he met his ex, Natalie.

I groan and as I get out of bed. I put on the sweatshirt that lies on the chair opposite the bed.

I slowly open the door and tiptoe down the hall to the bathroom, do what I need to do and then make my way to the kitchen.

It's a week day, so I have the house to myself and I don't open up my store for another few hours, so I'm thankful to have the space to myself, even though I'm invading someone else's home.

I start the Keurig and make myself a cup of coffee, after drinking a glass of water and taking some aspirin as I walk around Shaw's home. I've been here a million of times, but I'm not confident that I've recently looked around at what makes his home, a home.

The artwork from Mason hangs proudly on the fridge and along the wall beside the eat in kitchen area. In the living room, there are a few large black and white photos of still objects, mostly landscape images. There's a built-in bookshelf along one side of the wall where he has some random books and a million photo albums.

There are several photos of Mason, Shaw and Mason, photos of Shaw's parents and then several photos of Shaw and me through the years as well. One of the larger photos looks to be a candid photo of Shaw, Mason and me having a picnic, laughing together. I don't think I've seen the photo before now. My finger runs along the edge of the photo. We look like a family; we look so happy.

Does Shaw think of me as more than a friend?

Could I think of Shaw as more than a friend?

Looking at him in the photo, he's very attractive and knowing his character, makes him even more attractive.

I shake my head.

He's your best friend. Stop being ridiculous! I chastise myself and return to the kitchen to top off my coffee before getting in the shower to start my day.

Damn Sloane for putting those thoughts in my head.

My day is uneventful and half-way through when my staff comes in, I decide to leave and head to my apartment to get some things. I didn't grab any clothes and feel gross wearing yesterday's clothing, even though nobody noticed at the store. As I enter the apartment, I realize that I'm not as upset as I should be when someone's relationship falls apart.

I'm looking around the space as if I've never seen it before, with clarity.

While I chose this apartment, we both combined our furniture to make this place a home. What I see now, reflects none of that to me. I grab my suitcase and a few bankers boxes from the closet and once I have constructed the boxes; I place a few senti-mental knick knacks into the box, while I walk through the living room and the kitchen. I place the box beside the front door once it's full and take the suitcase to the bedroom.

The bed is unmade, and I see Colin's clothes on the floor beside his side of the bed. I look away from the bed and busy myself with the contents on my side of the closet. I pull down everything and fold it as neatly as possible, then place the hangers back on the rod. I move to the dresser and take my clothes out of there. Once my suitcase is full, I look under the bed and grab Colin's suitcase. Not caring that it doesn't belong to me, I put the rest of my clothes in the case then move to the bedside table on my usual side of the bed. I open the drawers and unceremoniously dump them into the case, one after the other, until I empty all three drawers. I look at the picture frame of Colin and I and face it down.

I look around the room and grab the art off the wall and

leave the room. I don't want any of the furniture, when I find a new place, I'll start fresh and not have any reminders of him.

I wheel both suitcases out of the apartment, down to the parking lot, and put them in the trunk of my car. I return to the house and begin filling up the reusable grocery bags with the food that I had recently purchased, leaving him with empty cupboards and an empty fridge.

Everything else in the apartment is just things, and things that can be replaced. I bring all the groceries down to my car and on my last trip, pick up the boxes beside the door and close the door on this part of my life. I pocket the key to remind myself to to go to the property managers office and remove myself from the lease.

FOUR

Summer

"HONEY! WE'RE HOME!" The front door slams and Shaw calls from the living room. Moments later, he walks into the kitchen just as I'm putting the chopped tomatoes into the salad that I prepared for dinner. He comes to my side, kisses the top of my head and peers into the salad bowl.

"What do we have here? Rabbit food, eh?" He says turning and walking over to the fridge.

He bends to get something out of the bottom drawer, and I can't help my eyes to follow the movement of his khaki pants tightening around his ass. His thick thighs stretch the fabric and I can see the indentation of his boxer briefs. He stands up and when he turns around, he catches me staring at him.

"What? Do I have something on my shirt?" He looks down and tries to figure out what I'm looking at, only I'm not staring at just one thing. I'm cataloging him, I've obviously checked out his butt and now I'm looking at the fabric stretching on his biceps.

I have never intentionally checked out Shaw's body before and come to think about it, I don't think I've ever seen him shirtless.

His loose-fitting work shirts never allow much to the imagination. Which now has me curious. His clothes lead one to believe that he's got a few extra pounds, maybe something that would resemble a dad bod, but then again, maybe he's hiding something spectacular under his clothing.

"Yo! Summer? You okay?" Shaw waves his hand in front of me, causing me to blink and snap out of my not so innocent thoughts of my best friend.

"Sorry, what?" My eyes focus and I turn to him with a smile.

"You're cooking dinner?" He asks, nodding to the bowl in front of me.

"Shoot, yes. I thought that since you're being cool with me staying here, that I would cook dinner. I have lamb in the slow-cooker and some pasta that Mason will eat for a side with the salad. If that's okay?"

"Sum, you know I'm shit at cooking. I'll eat whatever you put in front of me at any time," he smiles.

"Oh really?" I quirk an eyebrow, my mind going directly into the gutter.

I shake my head.

What has gotten into me?

"As long as it's not Brussel sprouts, how long until dinner is ready?"

"About twenty minutes," I say, looking at the clock above the stove.

"Perfect, I'll be right back." He says, turning on his heel. Before he leaves the kitchen entirely, he turns around. "I'm a dick, how are you doing?" He asks.

That's a loaded question. I'm thinking dirty thoughts about my best friend, as I'm cooking him and his son dinner.

"I'm doing fine, thanks." I reply.

He taps his knuckles on the wall, smiles and then mouths that he'll be right back.

Moments after Shaw is gone, Mason enters the kitchen.

"It smells yummy," he says, coming to my side.

I ruffle his hair as I normally do and smile down at him.

"Dinner is almost ready; do you need to go wash your hands?" I ask him.

"I don't know how." Mason says.

"Oh please, I'm not new here. Go wash your hands, buster," I say to him.

"Danger."

"Danger? What happened now?" Shaw asks walking back into the room, wearing a tight-fitting t-shirt that hugs his chest and thins out down his abdomen. He's wearing blue sweat shorts and I do what I can to tear my eyes away from him and not try to stare at him. I've seen Shaw casual plenty of times over the years, but suddenly my thoughts are running rampant and I'm thinking about him without clothes and feeling my heart beating faster as he nears.

"Danger. Auntie Summer hasn't cooked for us before. What if the house burns down?" Mason asks Shaw.

"Buddy, I think the only danger that is ever in store is when I'm cooking, Auntie Summer cooks very well, you'll see."

"What's for dinner?" Mason asks, turning to me.

"You're favorite," I reply with a smile while wiping my hands.

"Daddy doesn't let me have ice cream for dinner." Mason crosses his arms in front of his chest and pouts.

I bend down to his level and put my hand on his shoulder.

"If you eat all of your dinner, you might get dessert." I whisper to him.

"What kinds of dessert?" He leans in and loudly whispers as if we are sharing a secret.

"Only the special kind for you buddy!" I wink and then stand up.

"Should I be worried that the kid will be up all night?" Shaw asks.

"Never, now, if you could set the table, that would be amazing." I ask him.

He salutes me and then moves around me in the kitchen, grabbing everything that we will need for our feast.

Once everyone is seated and a plate is in front of them, I pick up my fork.

"Bon appetite." I say.

Mason digs into his pasta and does his best to make every forkful go into his mouth, he makes the adequate happy noises while eating and I look expectantly to Shaw for the same, but notice that he's shoveling his food into his mouth as if he was participating in a contest.

When dinner is over, Shaw leans back and pats his stomach.

"You impregnated me," he says while wiping his mouth with his other hand.

"What'd that mean daddy?" Mason looks to Shaw.

"Well, it means that Aunt Summer cooked us some really good food and my belly is happy."

"Auntie Summer, you pregnated me too, I love oodles!"

I laugh when Shaw sits forward. "Alright, I want you to go play for a bit. I'm going to clean up and then it's bath time, got it?"

"I can give him a bath," I offer.

"No, you chill. You made us dinner and I couldn't be more appreciative over a home cooked dinner,"

"But—"

"Summer, please. You're a guest here in the house, and more

importantly, you are my best friend, you don't have to do anything."

"I'll wear you down, mister." I playfully shake my finger at him.

"Oh, I bet." He wiggles his eyebrows.

Only I don't think we're thinking in the same manner.

FIVE

HIS HANDS ROAMED over the surface of my body, the bubbles from the soap leaving a trace of where he's touched me. When his hand reaches my thigh, his hands slowly move inward, and I can feel his fingers tips lightly grazing...

"SUMMER? UH, SUMMER?" My rampant thoughts are interrupted by Shaw's voice and the faint sound of the creaks of the door opening, "oh shit, I'm sorry, I should have knocked, I didn't think, I'll just, yeah, I'll see you later." The door slams and I'm frozen in place.

My chest is heaving while I slowly remove my hand from between my legs.

I suck in a deep breath and blink several times.

Did that really happen?

Ok, so Shaw just walked into the room while I was masturbating and caught me knuckles deep in a fantastic session. A session where I imagined he was lathering my body in the shower, and just as he was getting to the good part, the real Shaw appeared.

Do I go and face him? What do I say? I mean, touching yourself is a natural thing, everyone does it.

I decide to own up my womanhood and go talk to him. But first, I put on shorts and wash my hands.

I find Shaw in the kitchen washing a dish, a dish that is spotless. He's looking out the window above the sink into the backyard as he continues to make circular motions.

"Hey, umm, hi best friend," I say, leaning on the counter to his left.

Shaw jolts slightly at the interruption of his likely running rampant thoughts of what he may have walked in on. He turns off the water, wipes his hands on his shirt, then turns to face me.

"Listen, I'm sorry. I should have knocked, and I promise you that I didn't really see much, I mean, I saw stuff, but I—"

"Hey, no need to explain. For good measure though, care to leave your door open while you give yourself a tug later, that way this won't be so awkward?"

"Awkward? This isn't awkward," he shakes his head, looking everywhere but at me.

"Bull to the shit. You got to see my lady bits, you saw me diddling, and now you can't even look me in the eyes. I'm surprised though that it's taken us so long to walk in on one another in an indisposed situation," I smile. I am completely mortified that he saw me, but his cute embarrassment has me hoping that my joking will put him at ease.

"Yeah," is all that he says.

"We're both adults, and we know what sex is, along with the fact that we both have it, so let's be grown-ups about this and pound fists or something and then go on our merry little way," I offer him.

"Yeah, grown-ups, pounding of the fists," he blinks and then shakes his head. "I'm sorry, I really wasn't expecting to see all of you," he waves his hand up and down my body.

"Well, now you have. I'm telling you, if you strip right here and right now, we'd be even," I step forward and grab the hem of his shirt to playfully tug on it just as he steps back taking his shirt out of my grasp.

"Nope, nope, you don't wanna see this here. We're cool, we really are. No need to make things even, I think that would actually make me a little more self-conscience."

"What are you hiding under there? So what if you have a dad bod," I laugh.

"I do not," he protests.

"Okay then, show me?" I ask.

"Go away, you devil woman!" Shaw jumps away from me as my hands meet the counter that was behind him.

"Oh, don't worry, I will get you," I taunt him.

He leaves the room and as I walk through the living room; I turn off the lights, it's late anyway and I need to get to bed. I hear his bedroom door close and I laugh to myself.

"SO, did he see your good side?" Sloane asks, spinning herself around on the stool while I put books away on the layaway shelf behind the register.

"My good side? What would be my good side, he was basically looking up the barrel by the way the bed faces the door," I say with a roll of my eyes.

"Did you shoot out of the barrel for him?" she laughs.

"I hate you sometimes."

"No you don't. Trust me, you need a female in your life to talk about this stuff with, it's not like you can go and talk to Shaw about it."

"I tried," I reply.

"Omigod! What did you say?"

"I asked him what he thought of the show. No, I basically made a lame joke and then tried to maul him."

"Maul him? Were you still randy from the finger painting?"

"Gross, Sloane. You're a teacher, c'mon have better words that that!"

"My students don't play with finger paints, but I wouldn't doubt that your roommate is an expert," she wiggles her eyebrows.

"Again, gross. Shouldn't you be grading homework or something?"

"I did that during my free period. I'm all yours," she says with a grin.

"I would rather you go, you may scare my customers," I wave to the empty space.

"You mean your imaginary friends," she looks around, "what time is the book club tonight and what are they reading? Will they be bringing booze? Those book club ladies are a riot."

"They're reading some small-town romance by an indie author, and I think they always bring booze," I reply.

"Oh, my type of broads, you staying?"

"No, I have one of the staff manning the book clubs. I greet them and she stays until ten when they leave," I pull out my planner and look at the tentative schedule for the month.

"What time do they start?" Sloane questions.

"Same time as usual, seven. Do you want in on their club? I think you just need to join their Facebook group and accept whatever event that's in there. That's where all their information is," I tear a piece of scratch paper and write down their Facebook group name for her.

"I've got work to do, so unless you want to help me enter all these new titles into the POS system, go home, go do something meaningful with your time."

"You don't love me anymore," she pouts.

"I love you plenty, but I really do have work to do, and I wanna get it all done before I go home tonight."

"Speaking of which, you settling into Shaw's place, or are you looking for your own spot?" she asks and pulls her purse strap over her head to rest on her shoulder.

"I haven't thought that far ahead yet." I admit, "Shaw says that I can stay for as long as I need, so I wanted to give myself time, since I'm not in any rush."

"And so you can keep giving him peep shows, I got you," she walks towards the door waving and exiting my shop while I shake my head.

I didn't dispute that. Did I?

SIX

SHAW

I CAN'T GET the image out of my head and I really don't want to. It was the most surprising, yet a welcome one that I have experienced in quite some time. I'm not going to lie and say that I've never pictured Summer naked, or that she and I were wrapped up in one another. It's something that is reoccurring, especially when I need to get off without porn.

She was on her back, her hair was up in a messy bun on the white pillow, with her knees bent and her feet planted. Her hand was between her legs, she ran her finger along her delicious folds first then inserted one finger and removed it. Her finger was coated in her juicy wetness as she brought the same finger to her clit. Her other hand was squeezing her breast, her eyes were closed, and her mouth was parted.

She didn't know how much I saw, but I saw enough to add into my spank bank for years to come. I stood there in shock and awe, and then promptly went downstairs to begin washing dishes to busy myself.

I knew Summer would come downstairs and she would want to talk, and I almost stripped when she mentioned making things even. She thought that I was uncomfortable; I wasn't.

What I was though was extremely turned on and I didn't want to show her the massive erection she gave me. I wanted to walk into her bedroom, push her legs further apart and dine on her pussy. But she's my best friend and doesn't think of me like that, so a man must do what he has to do and stand in my shower with one hand on the tile and the other on my cock for the second day in a row.

That's where I am right now. The water is cascading down on the back of my neck as I squeeze my cock and envision my best friend with her fingers back in her pussy.

This time, her eyes are on me as she plays with herself as I pull up on my shaft roughly. My teeth are grinding, I clench my eyes tight as I watch her in my mind fucking herself. I feel my balls tighten and a moment later hot spurts of come are splayed on the tile.

As if timed out, I hear Mason screaming. No time to relish in the aftershocks of my orgasm, I grab a towel as I run out of the shower, through my bedroom and down the hall to Mason's room. Tightening the towel at my hip, I bend over Mason's bed as he throws himself from side to side, crying out. I gently wake him, and when his eyes finally settle on me, he leans up and hugs me.

"You okay, little man?" I whisper into his hair.

"What happened?" His little voice asks, as Summer appears in the doorway out of breath.

"I think you were having a bad dream, but you're okay now," I pull back and look him over.

"Okay, Daddy. I'm tired," he says, leaning back in bed.

"Go back to sleep, night kid."

"Night daddy, you need a towel," he mumbles as he turns over onto his stomach and proceeds to fall back asleep.

I keep the door halfway closed and then come face to face with Summer in the hallway.

"Sorry if he woke you up," I offer her.

"Shit, I think my heart leapt out of my chest. I was passed out on the couch, but whew," she places the back of her hand across her forehead as her eyes take me in. "Um, Shaw?"

"Yeah?" I say.

"You're only wearing a towel," she points out.

"Yeah, sorry. I was just in the shower," I reply sheepishly.

"You've got abs, and you've got a vee, and oh my, I should sit down," she leans against the wall and drifts down it until she's sitting on the floor.

"Are you okay? You're acting weird," I say bending a little, while adjusting the towel so I don't give her a show.

"Confession time," her eyes widen, "I just wasn't expecting to see so much of you flesh-wise and well, I just saw the twig and berries I think, and I think you should have prepped me a little," she rambles.

"How would I have prepped you?" I say with a grin.

"You need a sign following you or something."

"Oh yeah, and what would this sign say?" I play along.

"It would read 'Warning, hot bod alert', then I think I would have been properly informed," she shakes her head.

"Summer, get off the floor." I stand up and hold my hand out to her.

"I don't think I can, I'm just going to sit here for the next several days."

"Quit being weird."

"I just realized that you have a six-pack and have been hiding all this for all these years, this is going to take a while, plus, I got a glance at the goods, I think."

"So then, we're even," I reply, going into my bedroom and laughing as I close the door behind me.

On the other side of the door, I hear her groan and a thump. I return to my bathroom and remove the towel and step into the boxers that I had ready.

Either she was clearly affected just now, or I could have been imagining it all.

SEVEN

I RACK my brain trying to figure out if I've ever seen Shaw without his shirt off? Maybe back in the day, but back then I wasn't particularly thinking of him in the ways that I've started to as of recently.

He wears clothes that hide his amazing physique and now I just want him to walk around the house shirtless.

Is that too much to ask for?

It's not that I've been avoiding Shaw, because I haven't, we just haven't been in the same room together for too long, or at home at the same times this week. But ever since I saw what I saw, I've been keeping to myself to try and really figure out these thoughts that I've been having about him.

I had just gotten out of a relationship, why would I entertain getting in another one so soon and potentially ruining years of friendship.

But friends to lovers is so perfect, it's the perfect type of romance. A friendship is a good foundation to build a romantic relationship on, you already have the important parts of the person known, then comes the fun and exploring parts.

It's as if I'm trying to convince myself.

Mason is with his mom this weekend and I'm home alone making myself a sandwich, when I hear a female voice enter the house, followed by Shaw's. They are both talking animatedly until they come into the kitchen. I look down at my outfit and since I wasn't expecting anyone to come home, I'm wearing short shorts and a white tank with a dark bra.

"Oh, who's this? You have a house cleaner?" she asks looking at me.

Why would she assume that I am a house cleaner, what if I was his girlfriend? Do I not look like girlfriend material?

"God, no," Shaw says quickly. "This is one of my best friends. She lives here. Summer meet Connie. Connie, meet Summer," I wipe my hand on the towel beside me and step forward to shake her hand.

She loosely shakes and gives me a fake smile.

"How do you two know one another?" I ask, resting my hip on the counter casually.

"Oh, we went out a few times," Connie replies, then runs her finger along Shaw's shoulder. "But this guy has been playing hard to get, so I talked him into lunch today."

"Yeah, she got me," he shrugs with a strange look on his face.

"Well, cool. I'm just gonna finish up making my sandwich and I'll scoot out of your way, pretend I'm not even here," I turn and say.

Connie turns to Shaw and presses herself against him. *Hussy.*

She threads her fingers into his short hair and leans up to whisper something into his ear. He mumbles something that I can't hear as I slap the turkey on my bread and then quickly spin around to rinse my butter knife.

I look up to see Shaw's hands on her hips, gently pushing her away and taking a step back himself. I rush past them and head toward my room.

His date is annoying, and I can tell by the look on his face that he's thinking the same thing. It's awkward, especially the way she looked me over, the way she spoke to me, and the way she got even closer to Shaw, as if she had a claim to him. It's been awhile since I've seen him with another woman and with my newfound feelings, I can say that I didn't like it.

She's definitely not the type of woman that I've ever seen Shaw with, which is rare, and he looked a little uncomfortable as well. He probably had chicks over all the time before I moved in, it's not like I was over here all the time. I haven't known of him dating anyone recently but it's his house and he can bring home anyone that he wants; so, I shouldn't be upset or uncomfortable. Except I am, because I'm having these feelings about him.

A knock interrupts my thoughts of confusion and Shaw peaks his head in, but his eyes are closed.

"You decent?" he asks.

"I'm always decent," I reply, setting down my sandwich on the plate on my lap.

"Just didn't want to interrupt any special time," he smiles while he sits at the end of the bed. "I'm sorry about Connie."

"Why?" I ask.

"She was rude to you," he shrugs.

"Girls are always rude to one another when they're on the hunt, it's okay," I reply.

"While that could be true, no one treats *you* rudely. I only went out to lunch with her because she nonchalantly asked mid-conversation and I didn't even notice, then I was stuck and couldn't back out."

"So, you're not interested in her?" I ask.

"God no, she's vapid. I would prefer to stay as far away from her as possible," he shakes his head.

"You looked like you didn't mind the attention," I breathe.

"I don't want her attention, Summer," he says pointedly.

"Oh, okay," I pick up my sandwich and take a bite out of it, not sure what else to do.

"You seemed uncomfortable in the kitchen, everything okay?"

"Yep, I'm good. Just surprised, that's all," I reply.

He observes me quietly and then stands up.

"Listen, I want to have a BBQ tomorrow. It's the end of the year, it's finally nice enough, and I turned the pool heater on last week. I want you there, and if you want to invite anyone that I haven't already of our friends, that's cool."

"Yeah, okay, sure," I nod.

"And tonight, let's have a movie night, yeah? Since you moved in, we haven't just hung out."

"That sounds nice," I say with a smile.

He grins back at me, leaves the room, leaving me to my sandwich and my running thoughts.

———

POPCORN, Netflix, fuzzy socks, and my best friend. I couldn't ask for anything more, however my stomach is doing flips and I'm not really concentrating on the movie. We're watching the hit movie on Netflix with Sandra Bullock, blindfolds, and a cage with birds in it. A few times, Shaw and I reach into the popcorn bowl at the same time and I would minorly freak out in my head.

But now, the popcorn is done, and I have nothing to fumble with. Shaw's hand is relaxed along the back of the couch, just behind my head. It's normal, nothing he never did before, but now I'm mentally telling him to drop his hand and let it land on my shoulder. To pull me into him and snuggle me.

"Can you pause it really quick?"

"Didn't you just go to the bathroom?" he asks.

"You know that I have a delicate bladder, I take one sip of liquid and bam! Full bladder," I say as if it's normal.

"Hurry up, woman," he playfully taunts.

I return a moment later and sit back down, Shaw reaches forward and grabs the remote, plops back down on the couch, then rearranges himself so that his thigh is touching my knee as I sit crisscrossed on the couch.

He's touching me! My brain squeals.

Shaw's hand rests on top of my knee casually, as if it's no thang, and suddenly goosebumps erupt over my skin and I think that I've stopped breathing all together.

"Ready?" Shaw looks to me and asks.

I can't manage to say anything, my mouth is dry, my heart is beating a million beats a minute and I'm afraid to break this moment, so I nod.

The movie resumes, my back is ramrod straight and I can feel myself swallowing. After ten minutes of this, Shaw pauses the movie again and then looks at me.

"What is wrong?"

"What do you mean?" I ask quietly.

"You're stiff as a board, you're acting weird, are you okay?"

"Yep, I'm good. I'm fine, better than fine. I'm great," I say, probably a little too eagerly.

"Relax a little, we're watching a movie," he playfully jabs me in the side.

I take a deep breath and relax into the couch. Shaw's hand stays on my knee and I do not know what happened in that movie.

EIGHT

THE WEATHER IS PERFECT, and I've got enough food and beverages to feed an entire town. Summer is busy in the kitchen sipping on some colorful fruity drink that Sloane made her and making a charcuterie board that she insisted on making for the party and ignoring me for some strange reason.

Last night during the movie, she has been distant and I'm not exactly sure how to interpret any of it.

I leave a sign on the door telling guests to go through the side gate which leads into the backyard where the party will be focused. Thankfully, guests won't have to travel far for a bathroom since there is one in the back mudroom that takes you into the backyard from the house.

People are slowly showing up and I've started mingling around with some local friends that I've known for years and a few teachers who like to socialize with one another.

Throughout the day, Summer and I have continued to be on

opposite sides of the party. She's had Sloane and one other woman hanging with them on the far side of the pool by the tiki bar for the majority of the time, and when I walked over to join in on their conversation as I mingled from group to group, Summer would be quiet in a nervous kind of way. By dusk, the party has dwindled down and only a few people remained. Summer stands in the kitchen with Sloane laughing when I walk in, with a beer in my hand and my buddy Luke trailing behind me.

Luke and I know one another from high school, he's a hotshot business man now and hard to figure out. Sloane perks up immediately at seeing us, then pops a chip in her mouth.

"Shaw, good you're here. Summer and I were talking about relationships," Sloane slurs leaning on her elbow bent over the counter.

"Um, alright."

"Let's not bring Shaw into whatever game you're planning," Summer says with a slight slur as well.

How much have they been drinking?

"No, include me," I smile, setting my beer on the counter and leaning back against the fridge.

"All right. Have you had a kiss that just blew your mind? Like a spark goes through you and you feel like you've found your person?" Sloane asks.

I wasn't expecting that question; I take a moment and think back to anyone that I've dated. From my first kiss with Becky Hanson, to the girlfriend back in my junior year of high school that I lost my virginity to, Marie, Mason's mom, I don't recall any bolts of lightning.

"I think it's obvious that I haven't had a kiss to make me think that she is my person, but I would like to think that every kiss has the potential. Every kiss could be something great."

"Oh, wow. That's a really excellent answer." Sloane stands

straight, smiles, then claps her hands together excitedly. "I've got a fantastic idea."

Summer stands up straight and suddenly looks nervous.

"Sloane, let's get you to bed, come with me?" She pleads.

"No, no, no. I think this would be fun. Okay. Shaw, you and I have never kissed, right?" Sloane starts.

"Um, no—why would we have?"

"I don't know for funsies, and you have never kissed Summer, right?" she asks.

"He hasn't kissed me either, thanks for asking," Luke says with a grin.

"I'll get to you in a second, handsome," Sloane practically purrs at him.

"What are you getting at?" I ask her.

"What if Summer was your person, or what about me?"

Summer crosses her arms.

"So, what are you proposing?" I ask, stepping forward.

"I'm saying, let's experiment," she grins widely as Summer covers her eyes and groans.

I'm not sure how to react to any of this, but I'm curious to do some extra research, you know, for science.

"Well, if it's going to lead me closer to finding *the one*, I should probably make sure to not pass up you two, right?" I shrug.

"You can just ignore her, we don't need to do any of this," Summer holds up her hands.

"Is this party turning into an orgy?" Luke asks just as Sloane shushes him.

"I'll go first," Sloane says as she walks around the corner and comes to stand right in front of me. She winks, then leans up and presses her lips against mine. The kiss holds but doesn't deepen. A second later, she pulls back.

"Such a shame, you're husband material," Sloane shakes her head. "Okay, Summer, it's your turn."

"We really don't have to," she says to me.

"One kiss, that's all," Sloane says.

"When is it my turn? I haven't met my person yet," Luke says.

"Luke, I don't think you're ready to meet your person," Sloane says.

"And why is that?" he crosses his arms and asks.

"I don't think that you are ready to find out that I am your person," Sloane smirks. "But maybe we should give Summer and Shaw some privacy for their kiss?"

"Why, we didn't give you any privacy, and that kiss was quick." Luke defends.

"I think it's just something that we should do," Sloane shrugs.

"Fuck it, you don't have to go anywhere," Summer steps around the counter, comes to stand in front of me and gives me a chaste kiss on the lips.

"Na uh! That doesn't count, you need to give it a chance, let it marinate," Luke says.

"Agreed, I think we need to give this a shot," I add.

"Oh God, not you too?" Summer puts her hands on her hips.

"It's for science," I grin widely. My stomach is doing flips in the anticipation of kissing Summer.

She sighs loudly and I look at her, giving her puppy dog eyes.

"You're giving into silly drunk games, you realize that, right?" Summer whispers leaning into me with her hands on her hips.

"We'll chalk it up to being drunk," I shrug with a smile.

"Are you drunk?" she asks.

"I'll never tell," I lean in and whisper back.

"I've never seen anyone debate over whether or not to kiss as much as you, Summer. Just get on with it," Sloane says.

"Alright, for science," Summer steps forward again.

We are standing toe to toe; I place my hand nervously on her waist and pull her toward me. I lean my head down as she angles her head up. My lips cover her warm lips as her hands rest on my hips. I can feel her fingertips digging into my skin as she opens her mouth, my tongue slides in and explores hers. I suddenly have an awareness of my heartbeat as Summer's body relaxes into mine.

She kisses me back, fiercely. Our kiss deepens and I'm swept away in the moment. I'm not sure how long I stood there kissing Summer, my best friend in my kitchen, but I'm not caring at this moment. From the way that Summer is lost to the kiss, just as I am, I'm pretty sure that neither is she.

Luke clears his throat from behind us, disrupting our moment, and as we pull away from the magnetic moment I feel a need to pull her back into my arms.

Summer wipes her lips and looks up at me. Her eyes focus on mine and she blushes.

"I think I need to change my panties," Sloane says, breaking the moment.

"Yeah, that was super hot, I felt like I shouldn't have been watching," Luke says.

I wish that they weren't either. Perhaps we wouldn't have stopped kissing.

Now, she is looking everywhere but at me.

Summer hiccups and covers her mouth in embarrassment.

"So, that was pretty hot, I mean wow," Sloane says from behind me.

"Sure as shit was," Luke agrees, "in fact, I think I've got a slight chub from watching that. I kind of feel like a voyeur and that was something that I shouldn't have seen, but I'm damn glad that I did."

NINE

Summer

MY KNEES ARE WEAK, my heart is pounding, and I have the urge to jump up on Shaw to continue that kiss. But I'm not sure where he stands, hell I'm not sure where I stand. My thoughts are fuzzy, and I don't know if it's the aftereffects of the intense kiss that we just shared or the alcohol running through my blood. I'm not sure where to look, but I can't bring myself to look at Shaw.

"You two sure that you've never kissed before?" Sloane asks.

Neither of us say anything, but finally our eyes meet. I see heat in his stare and can feel the blush covering any exposed skin.

"Hello? Earth to Summer? Earth to Shaw?" Sloane steps between us, breaking the intense moment, and my eyes fixate on her.

"Hi," I say quietly.

"You okay there?" she asks.

"Yeah, I'm fine, I'm going to—I'm going to go to bed, I'm

beat and yeah," I walk out of the kitchen narrowly missing a wall. As I turn into the hallway, Shaw's voice stops me.

"Wait," he calls. When I turn around, his eyes are pleading for me to stay.

"It's been a long day, I'm tired," I lie.

"Sum?" he whispers as my hand grips the doorknob and I freeze. I slowly turn towards him.

"Can we just talk about this tomorrow?" I ask him.

"I can't. I don't want to let time to go by not address what just happened in there," he says.

"It was a silly game that Sloane conjured up, let's chalk it up to that," I tell him. "Remember, we're drunk."

"That's bullshit and you know it. You felt what I did," he says, stepping closer so that he is towering over me. He pulls my hand in his and laces our fingers together. My eyes capture each second as if in slow-motion.

"Shaw," I say.

"Look at me, Summer?" he asks, and I do as he requests without hesitation.

"That in there wasn't a game. It felt real to me. Please tell me that you felt it too?" he asks.

I say nothing, but I nod my head slowly.

"So, I wasn't imagining that? The intensity?" he asks.

"No," I whisper.

"I need to get Sloane and Luke out of here," he says abruptly.

"What?"

"Don't fall asleep, please whatever you do, do not fall asleep on me," he says before turning and walking around the corner.

I sigh and open the door to the bedroom. I sit on the edge of the bed and fall onto my back with a thud, bouncing slightly on the mattress.

What happens now? Do we pretend the kiss never happened? Do we go about business as usual?

I touch my lips and stare at the ceiling, remembering the feeling of his lips on mine. How at first the kiss was tentative. How the kiss deepened and how amazing that it felt. Never did I think that I would have been drunkenly standing in the kitchen kissing my best friend, and never before did I think that I would like it so much and want to kiss him repeatedly.

A light tap on my open door alerts me to Shaw's presence.

"May I come in?" he asks from the doorway.

"Sure," I reply, sitting up. He sits beside me, angles his knee and faces me.

"What are you thinking?" he asks.

"A million different things," I admit.

"Good things or bad things?"

"Both," I reply.

"Is it bad if I want to kiss you again?" he asks surprising me.

My head swings his way at his words. "What?"

"Confession time," he says. "I've wanted to kiss you since the day that we met."

My eyes go wide, and my mouth goes dry at his confession.

"Why is this coming out now?" I ask him.

"I've wanted to kiss you since we met, and here we are several years later, and I did. And like I said, I want to kiss you again. But I'm struggling with what's going on in your mind," he says.

"It's a mixture of thoughts. Like complicated thoughts, questions and stuff."

"Well, maybe I can help you with the questions, and hopefully that will uncomplicate things," he offers.

I gulp, take a deep breath and mimic his position on the bed.

"What does this do to our friendship, friends generally don't kiss friends?"

"Sometimes, the best relationships stem from a friendship. In order to be in a relationship, you have to have a foundation," he answers like an expert. As if this is something he's practiced several times in the mirror.

"We just kissed and now we're talking about relationships, gah!" I lay back on the bed and cover my eyes with my arm.

"We're talking things out. Don't panic. Tell me this, have you ever thought of us as more than just friends?"

A pregnant pause seems to last forever in the room. I pull my arm away from my eyes.

"Confession time," I say. "Yes, here and there over the years and recently."

"Recently?" he asks.

"Yeah, recently," I admit.

He nods and looks to mull over my confession.

"You have been a little jittery," he says with a smirk. He moves up on the bed and lies on his back so he's on my level.

"Shaw?" I whisper.

"Yeah, Summer?"

"You can kiss me again," I tell him. He leans up on his elbow and smiles down at me. With his fingers, he moves the hair off of my forehead.

"You're beautiful," he whispers.

I smile in return as he leans down. His face is inches away from mine as I close my eyes and open myself up to the idea of kissing Shaw without provocation.

Our lips touch and instantly I open up for him. His lips cover mine as our tongues seek out one another and once they touch, I feel a tingling sensation in my stomach at the movement. My hand moves to cup Shaw's jaw and to pull him closer.

Time stands still as my hand moves from his jaw down his neck to his shoulder to pull him over me. He comes willingly, never breaking the kiss as he now hovers over my body. My heart is beating rapidly as my hand moves around his front and to the end of his shirt. My fingertips touch his skin and I feel goosebumps erupt on his skin under my touch. I feel the quick intake of breath that he masks during the kiss, then he deepens the kiss.

Another moment passes and Shaw pulls back. His desire blatant on his handsome face as he breathes heavily.

"Was that too much?" he asks.

"No, not at all."

"What do you want to do, Summer?" he asks, leaning down and gently kissing my cheek, just beside my ear and down the column of my neck.

"I don't want you to stop doing this," I say in a breathy sigh, arching my neck to allow him more space to lay his soft kisses that are driving me wild.

"I don't want to stop either, but I think we've both been drinking and should continue this tomorrow when we're both sober, is that okay?"

"But you wanted to talk?"

"And we did. I think that this can be the start of something, something absolutely soulful and amazing. I want you to go to sleep thinking about what you want, and we can talk about it over breakfast. How does that sound?" he asks.

"I can do that," I say with a smile.

"Good, sweet dreams, Summer," he stands up, does a slight bounce on his feet as I stand as well, I walk over to the door to my bedroom.

"Where are you going?" he asks.

"Bathroom," I reply.

"Oh right," he nods.

"Did you think that I was following you?" I put my hand on my hip.

He looks embarrassed and stutters as I walk down the hall to the main bathroom across from Mason's room and disappear inside.

Shaw is standing against the wall outside of his bedroom when I emerge. I almost stop in my steps but continue forward anyway.

"Good night, Shaw," I reply, lingering as I slowly past him.

He reaches out and grabs my wrist after I pass and pulls me to him.

"I want one more kiss before going to sleep," he whispers against my lips. He kisses softly, his tongue lashing out lightly, but this kiss is sweet and longing, not rushed, not full of magnetism and definitely showing that there will be more of this to come.

TEN

Summer

I'M SITTING in my room avoiding Shaw and not answering the phone as Sloane calls me every five minutes.

I know that after those kisses, I shouldn't be avoiding him, and I know that we need to discuss what happened. While we talked a little before he kissed me again, I need to gather my thoughts and really think about the consequences of what this relationship could be.

While he made good points last night about foundation and blah, blah, blah—I need to think heavily about if this is a risk that I'm willing to take.

I lean up on my knees and do what I can to reach from the edge of the bed to the desk that sits across from it, as I'm reaching, too lazy to actually get up, my knee slips and I let out a high-pitched scream as I fall face first on the carpet.

Dazed and confused, with my ass and feet up in the air, the bedroom door swings open and Shaw runs in. I manage to turn my head that is currently pressed against the plush fabric of the carpet and see his feet mere inches away from me.

"Summer, what are you doing?" he asks.

"Yoga," I reply.

"I think you're doing it wrong," he says, bending down and trying to look at me.

"Do you think that you can help me up? I'm afraid that if I try, I will injure myself, and that would be an embarrassing story to tell to the emergency room doctors."

"I'd love to know what you could come up with," he says standing, and then stepping beside the bed. His arms reach around my waist and he pulls me up and plops me back to a sitting position.

"Thank you," I reply sheepishly.

"Nice underwear," he says with a smirk. "What were you doing, really?"

"I was trying to get that notebook," I point over the desk.

Shaw reaches for the notebook and hands it to me. "Think we can do breakfast or something in a bit? You know to talk and shit?"

"And shit?" I look at him.

"I'm nervous, this is a whole new ball field here and I'm not sure how you really feel now that you've slept on it all. All I can tell you is that kissing you last night was like a dream and I don't want to wake up from it."

Breath. Stolen.

"Sure, I'll be out in a bit," I reply quietly.

He leaves the room and I've got the notebook now in my lap. I create two columns; a PRO column and a CON column. I wouldn't say that this is the best way to go about deciding the future of Shaw and I. However, it's a start, and it could help me wrap my head around the whiplash of my thoughts.

Pro. We know each other's quirks already and the getting to know one another factor is easier.

Con. We lose the ability to get to learn the quirks by trial and error.

But is that really a con? Or is that a blessing?

Pro. I already know that he's a good guy.

Con. He comes with a crazy ex.

I shouldn't hold that against him.

Pro. We know of one another's past.

Pro. He's an amazing, caring, and thoughtful father.

Con. He's a dad, so I don't get all of him.

I shouldn't hold that against him, either.

Pro. He's a really good kisser.

Pro. Built in best friend into relationship

Pro. We can take our friendship into a deeper level.

Con. We could risk eight years of friendship

Pro. He's seen me at my worst, and he's seen me at my best.

Pro. Awkward parent moment, not possible. Our families already love one another.

Con. If it doesn't work, what happens to our circle of friends?

Pro. I don't have to get dressed up for him.

Pro. Shaw already knows how to cheer me up

Pro. We already know one another's expectations for dating and what we want out of life.

Con. Those expectations are fun to learn. Maybe there are new things that we can learn?

I look at my list and notice that there are a more significant amount of Pro's than the latter. I could continue adding to the list, but I'm not sure if that is needed. The major Con though, that still sticks out to me is about risking the entire relationship.

I get off the bed and grab my shorts to slip on. I head out

into the kitchen in search of Shaw, to no avail. I turn around and head towards his bedroom. His door is open, and I hear the shower running from his bathroom, and go back to the kitchen. I should make some coffee. If there's more conversation to be had together, I'm going to need it.

ELEVEN

Shaw

EVERYTHING THAT HAPPENED last night shifted my entire understanding of the world. When she admitted that she's thought about us as more than friends on more than one occasion, it took everything inside of me to not jump up and start doing cartwheels around the house. But, it's a good thing that I didn't, since I haven't done a cartwheel in years.

I'm showered and ready to prepare the best breakfast that one could ask for after a day like yesterday. A day of cat and mouse, then a tremendous revelation that there could be something more to the friendship that we've had for so many years.

She's standing at the counter in the kitchen, both hands cradling a steaming cup of coffee. She's in her favorite pair of shorts and a sweatshirt, her long caramel hair is in a half-fast bun on her head. She's blowing at the coffee in her hands, staring out the window over the kitchen sink that overlooks the backyard, deep in thought.

I sneak up beside her, place my hand lightly on her hip, and lean to the cupboard beside her. She jolted slightly at the touch and then settled into it with an audible breath.

"Sorry," I whisper to her. "I wasn't sure if you were meditating or something, you looked zoned out."

"If I was meditating, you shouldn't have touched me and walked into my personal space, that would be so un-Zen like of you and you would have busted up my setting the intentions for the day into the universe," she grins.

"Funny, you're saying so many new age types of things that I wouldn't be surprised that you did meditation."

"And if I did?"

"I think that would be awesome. I can't be still long enough to do it, so I give more power to those that can... do you?" I ask.

"I do, before bed, it usually helps me sleep better," she replies.

I hold up my fist. "That deserves a solid pound," I say with a smile.

"Are you making fun of me?" she looks at me with a confused look.

"Not one bit, I think it's cool. Anyway, how are you this lovely morning?"

"Tired, remind me to not do day drinking again, I don't think my body recuperates as it once did," she rubs the back of her neck.

Panic flows through my body, "Do you, do you remember last night?" I ask her with caution.

She blushes, nods, and her eyes dart to me while she bites her bottom lip. I set the cup on the counter and take the step to her and pull her against me.

She's standing with her hip against me and easily leans her head against my shoulder as my arms envelope her as if we've stood like this many times before. I feel her take in a deep breath.

"I want to cook you breakfast," I say with my chin on top of her head. Feeling her head nod, I kiss the top of her head, smile and release her.

"Waffles sound good?" I ask.

"Sounds perfect," she says, stepping away and moving to the other side of the counter to get out of the kitchen.

"So," I begin.

"So," she mimics.

"About last night," I say. "What are your thoughts there?"

"Man, that's quite a loaded question," she says heavily.

"I know, but it should be discussed, and I don't want it to just be swept under the rug."

"No, I know. But we have eight years of friendship, what about that?" she asks, setting down her cup.

"I think that is a pretty good foundation," I answer.

"What if something more happens with us and it doesn't work out? How would the friendship survive that?"

"We don't know that it won't work out. We would need to trust in taking the risk and seeing what could happen. I'm not telling you that I have the answers to it all, not by any means. But I've always told myself that if the opportunity presented itself, that I would take the leap," I admit. "I'm afraid that if something happens between us that sleeping together or whatever would make things different. I'm scared to lose you, and that's a possibility if a relationship together doesn't work out. I can't tell you what will happen in the future, but I can tell you this—I will undeniably do what I can to be your perfect match, or we can just go along back to our friendship as if nothing ever happened." I shrug.

"You said last night that you've wanted to kiss me from the start, why didn't you?" she tilts her head in question.

"I wasn't clear if you were interested, then we fell into the friends zone pretty quick and I was resigned to the fact that at least I had you in my life and that was better than not.”

“I see,” she nods, her thumb outlining the rim of her cup.

“You said you’ve thought about me as more than a friend from time to time?” I ask, hoping she will elaborate.

“Gosh, this is so embarrassing,” her head falls into her hands.

“What is?” I ask, mixing the waffle ingredients into the mixing bowl.

“Talking about this, with you, it’s very adult of us.”

“Well we’re adulting well then,” I look up and smile at her. “So?”

“When we first met, I had a slight crush. But like you said, we became friends and then yeah. But recently, ugh, do I really have to tell you this?” she covers her eyes and peeks out through the cracks.

“No, but *now* I really want to know,” I say.

She inhales deeply and then looks up, demanding my attention.

“I went out with Sloane, and she brought you up, and it was like a veil was lifted and suddenly I was seeing you in a different light, the same light that I did when we first met, but the older version of you. I noticed little things that I don’t think that I did before, and yeah.”

I have finished mixing everything and I’m blown away from her confession.

“Confession time?” I ask and proceed when she nods, “I’ve never not noticed those little things, I’ve pined after you for years,” I take a deep breath before saying this last bit, knowing that it’s a game changer. “And I really, really, really want to give in to whatever this is that’s brewing,”

“It’s coffee,” she says like the smart ass that she is.

“You know what I mean,” I move around the counter and

stand beside her, commanding her to turn and face me. "I want to see what amazing things can come out of a relationship, a romantic one, with you."

"That would be really confusing to Mason," she says for an excuse.

"That's not a reason for anything, Mason loves you and you're family, anyway. Good try though."

"What if it ruins our relationship?"

"Sometimes the best things come from taking a risk."

TWELVE

I AGREED to see what could happen between Shaw and me in a different capacity. I asked to take it slow, and he started with a slow and tantalizing kiss that made my heart beat faster and my toes curl. It made me want more and change my stance on starting slow.

We ate breakfast together and talked about the fact that Sloane's little game last night was purposeful, and I made a mental note to give her *the what for* later. While I'm happy with how the night and morning ended up, I'm also terrified.

It's a 'should we or shouldn't we' kind of worry. I'm hoping that Shaw and I diving into something new like this will not end in a disaster. After breakfast, I'm getting ready for work and Shaw is expecting his ex to bring Mason home. We've decided that we will not make a big deal about the change of direction of our relationship when Mason is here, when it feels right or if— we will figure out how to talk to him together.

My stomach is flipping when I change the closed sign on the

store to open and I turn on the lights. I go through the motions of opening and only after a few customers come and go, do my eyes widen.

Holy shit, at some point, I will do the Humpty dance with Shaw. Like the horizontal tango, the four-legged foxtrot. We will put the banana in the fruit salad. He will dip his stinger in my honeypot. Oh my God. I will see him naked, intentionally.

I chug some of my water and look for something to keep me busy. I find the latest book delivery from a local independent author who will sign at the store next week. Perfect, I can set up the window display and create some flyers for the signing. I get to work first on the flyer and once I'm satisfied; I print.

I wheel over the book cart to the table front and center of the store once you walk in, and I unload the table with the various children's books to move to a different space. I run over to the romance section of the store, and browse the author names for more titles by the author. I notice my stock is low, so I leave what's there to stay on those shelves and pull my phone from my back pocket.

I press for the author's agent and request an expedited order of some of her backlog titles, then resume to create a book tower with the newest release which will be the centerpiece of the table. As I'm bending to grab a few more books from the boxes, the door opens, Shaw walks through the door and gives me a smile that would melt my panties off. I awkwardly stand up and as I do, my hip nudges the table and my book tower tumbles.

"Ugh," I groan.

"Can I help you reassemble the stack?"

"No, thank you. It was a book tower, but I can figure that out later. What's up, what are you doing? Where's Mason?"

"Marie last minute texted me asking if it was okay if he came over around three today, her mom had planned something for them and forgot it wasn't Marie's time," he shrugs.

"Well, that was nice of you," I smile.

"Am I being too nice? I mean, shouldn't I be a little firmer with her and make sure that she keeps to the schedules?" he asks.

"Confession time?" I start, "I never liked her, so I would be the worst person to answer that."

"That wasn't a confession. That was public knowledge," he winks.

It's true. I never masked my distaste for her. I'm not sure if it was because she was with Shaw and deep down, I wanted to be that person. Or if I just didn't like her as a person. But she was very vocal in her disliking me as well. She wouldn't let Shaw and I hang out together and she would always call him when she knew I was around, and she wasn't. Although her over protection didn't seep into keeping her extra-curricular a secret. She was having a very public relationship when Shaw was out of town, as the only teaching job available was forty miles away. He would stay here during the weekends and during the week to ease his commute, he would stay in a shabby studio across the street from the elementary school that he was working at. Her affair with her now current boyfriend didn't stop her from remaining the ever vigilant and over-possessive girlfriend with Shaw. She accused him of hooking up while he worked there, which was the last straw that unfolded her own affair. By this time, Mason was only a one-year-old and his parents were separated. They worked out a small custody agreement that gave Shaw time to spend with his son, and as Mason got a little older, they expanded some of the time spent with him as Marie started school again and had less time for Mason—more time to make sure she could dedicate to concentrating on school.

"Okay, so maybe not. Anyway, what are you doing here?" I ask, stacking some of the fallen books.

"I wanted to see if you wanted to do lunch?" he asks nervously.

"I can't leave, Tasha doesn't get here for another few hours."

"I can grab something and come back, I've got time," he offers.

I look at him and smile. This is nothing new, we'd have lunch together when time permitted, but now that we're venturing into this new avenue of our relationship, I'm nervous and unsure if we need to act differently, but I go with my gut.

"I would kill for a meatball sub," I say with enthusiasm to mask my nervousness.

"Yeah? Outstanding. I'll be back in twenty," he lingers as if trying to decide on something. He then leans in and chastely kisses me, grins, and then retreats from my shop.

While it wasn't a romantic kiss, it was a kiss from Shaw and something that I am still wrapping my head around. I touch my lips and smile to myself as I think how things have turned from friendship to navigating a relationship in a matter of hours.

Are we ready for that, for real?

I'm drifting around the shelves when my cell phone rings, I pull my phone from my back pocket and see Sloane's face on the screen. My finger hovers over the answer button and before I can answer, the shop door opens and Shaw waltzes in carrying a bag and a carrier with drinks. I silent the ringer and observe him.

With a wide smile on his face, he sets the items down on the counter and then looks around the shop for me. He doesn't see me standing off to the side as he walks in, making it easy to observe him unnoticed. He's carrying himself with confidence and looks to be in a good mood.

"Sum?" he calls out, looking around, but not seeing me behind the romance aisle.

I step into view with my phone still in my hand and a few books under my arm.

He looked from concerned, back to having a smile on his face when he sees me. He points to the food. "Time to stuff our faces," he announces.

I nod and grab a barstool for him to sit on. I move the one that sits behind the register desk and bring it to sit beside him as he places my sub in front of me.

"Wait, before we get started eating, and because my sandwich has pickles," he says pulling my stool to his. He leans in slowly and as our lips touch, I part my lips out of instinct and his tongue sweeps in. His hand moves to my waist and my hand goes to his knee. The kiss is intense and takes my breath away so that when we part, I'm in a daze and almost gasping for air.

"I don't know if I will ever get used to that," he whispers, pressing his forehead against mine.

"Thank you for remembering my pure hatred for pickles," I reply as he releases me, and we dive into our lunch in silence.

With my mind worrying still as to whether or not getting involved romantically is a good idea.

THIRTEEN

SHAW

I'M FLOATING on cloud nine right now. With a full stomach, I left the bookstore with one last kiss from Summer.

I'm cautious of moving too fast and scaring her, so the kiss was quick, and I made sure to not gross her out with any leftover taste of pickles from my lunch.

The time was nearing for my ex to drop off Mason for my week night with him, so I headed home with plenty of time to spare, just in case he came earlier.

Which was likely the smartest thing that I could have done, because Marie's car is parked in front of my house when I pull into the driveway.

As I step out of the car, I hear her say something to Mason, then slam her car door.

I turn to face her just as she stomps across my lawn, arms straight with closed fists.

"Hello Marie, how are you?" I say with a polite smile, knowing that it will piss her off.

"What the hell, Shaw? I've been waiting here for thirty minutes; you were supposed to be home!" she seethes.

"Woah, chill out. You said that he would be coming home at three. It's only two, if you were coming sooner or were waiting on me, it's not like you don't have my phone number. Instead of steaming in your car, approaching me like this in front of our son, you could have sent a 'hey, I'm here,' text or whatever," I say to her sternly.

"You were supposed to be home, Shaw," she says crossing her arms over her chest as if she's shoving them in a tight sleeve.

"I wasn't, and you don't get to dictate when I'm home. Now, we're going to motion for Mason, who is watching all of this interaction and you're going to leave politely, got it?" I say as calm as I can, despite my blood boiling.

She turns and waves to Mason, then turns back around to me.

"Don't speak to me like I'm a child," she demands.

"Then quit acting like one." I direct my attention to the miniature version of me that is running over. As he approaches, I smile and bend down in time for him to throw himself into my arms. "Hey bud, I missed you."

"Daddy, can we go swimming with auntie Summer?" he asks.

I hear Marie huff and I cut her a narrowed look. "Thanks Marie, I've got it from here." I say standing up with Mason's hand in mine. "Say bye to Mommy, pal."

She bends down and ruffles Mason's hair. "I'll see you tomorrow bud, yeah?"

"See you later, mama."

She stands up and without another word, she hurries back to her car.

"Why was mommy mad?" Mason looks up at me.

"Sometimes people are upset when they have to wait," I reply.

"Why were we waiting?" he asks innocently.

"I had to bring auntie Summer lunch. She won't be able to swim with us today, maybe later tonight if she isn't tired from work."

"But can we swim now?"

"Of course, let's go get our suits on."

THE FRONT DOOR slams and I hear Summer walk through the house. I'm standing over the counter cutting up a tomato for the burgers when she puts her purse on a chair and walks into the kitchen.

"Bad day?" I ask carefully minding my fingertips as I slice.

"Tasha never showed. She didn't call and when I tried to call her, the phone went straight to voicemail."

"Did your other employee come in?" I ask her setting the knife down.

"Yeah, after I called her, but she could only stay for a few hours, so will I need to go back in a few hours and stay until closing," she drops her head in her hands.

"Shitty, but at least you get to come home and eat before slaving away for another few hours," I smile.

"It's what a business owner does. Does your mom still want to volunteer at the shop? I can't afford to pay her, but having some more help during this time of year would be great."

"We can check and ask. I'm sure she's bored in retirement, Mason is in his room and I'm grilling, you want a double burger or a single?" I ask.

"I want a bath, some wine and a massage," she says in a sigh.

"But I will take a monster hug from Mason and a single, please?"

"Coming right up, and when you get back later, I'll see what I can do for the rest," I wink, take the plate of patties and head out towards the back through the mudroom to the BBQ.

I'll definitely assure she gets the other requests.

———

THE BOOKSTORE CLOSES at ten on weeknights, and it takes roughly ten minutes to get from there to the house. I uncork a bottle and place a glass on the bathroom counter beside it, start the water and place one of those weird chalky looking balls that women are all about nowadays on the edge of the bathtub. I turn on a few of those flickering candles that my mom got me a million years ago and turn off the lights.

By the time that I hear the front door open and close. The lights are still on in the main part of the house, so she will know that I'm still awake. I step out of the bathroom just as she steps into the hallway. She looks exhausted, yet happy to see me, which melts away any nerves that I had.

"Hey," I say as she walks into my arms. I hold her and feel her slump against me.

"Tonight was crazy, a book club full of drunk, rowdy women," she says into my shoulder.

"Well, I've got the perfect remedy for that," I steer her into the bathroom and when she realizes I've made her requests from earlier a reality she gasps, turns to me with her hand over her mouth and her eyes glistening.

"A massage will be made available to you after your soak if you want—but enjoy." I kiss her temple and push her forward into the space and close the door behind her.

She opens it immediately and I turn around, she throws

herself at me, my back slams against the wall and her lips are on mine. Then she retreats just as quickly as she came back into the bathroom.

I smile as I walk back to the living room, flip on the television, and sit on the couch. I'm not sure how quickly I fell asleep, but I feel Summer snuggle up to me and my arm automatically goes around her.

Her hand is caressing my chest in a mesmerizing motion, "thank you for my bath," she says.

"Welcome," I reply with my eyes still closed.

"I just wanted to thank you, go get to bed, you fall asleep here and you'll be hurting in the morning," she says attempting to sit up, but my hold stays firm on her.

"Just five more minutes," I say with a small smile.

"I will give you a purple nurple," she warns, placing her hand in position as my eyes shoot open.

"You wouldn't," I say.

"Don't believe me?"

"You won't."

"I totally would," she smiles devilishly.

"I could do the same to you too, you know," I say.

"You could, but you won't," she replies with confidence.

"Can we call it truce, I'm not entirely sure why you were threatening a purple nurple with me, and I'm too tired to figure it out right now."

She sat up and gave me space as I came to a full sitting position from my recently slumped over position. My arm goes around her, and I kiss her cheek. I'm not sure exactly how to take our friendship to a new level, other than with trial and error.

"Sum?" I begin as soon as I have her attention, I smile and spill out my thoughts. "I want to go at whatever pace that you do, but I want you to know that now that we've broken the seal that I'm all in, I'm ready for whatever you want and however."

"Broken the seal," she repeats, almost as if to herself. "Like when drinking and you hold in your pee in fear of breaking the seal and then having to go every ten minutes?"

"I'm not sure our relationship, in whatever fashion should be referred to as using the bathroom," I say.

"Well, you're the one who said it," she defends her train of thought.

"Okay, okay. So how about we ripped off the band-aid? Is that better?"

"So, what if the relationship was to get infected, we'd have to make sure that we use all the precautions that we could to keep the relationship," she winks, "healthy and strong. I like that better."

I shake my head at her explanation and understanding of the analogies.

"Yes, I'm not sure how your mind works sometimes, but yes. We're fresh, we're new, and we need to take care of one another."

"Like you would a cut," she nods.

"If that's what you want to go with, yes. Anyway, what I was originally trying to say, is we'll go at your pace. If you want slow, I can do slow and if you want, well whatever you want—I will go along with it."

"And what if I want to get freaky right here and right now?" she asks with a devilish smile.

My heart skips a beat and my mouth goes as dry as the desert. I clear my throat and smile.

"I would take you to my bedroom and remove your clothes and do whatever you wanted me to. If you want to get freaky, then we can. But when Mason is here, we have to be a little more cautious, at least until he knows about us."

"I was just testing you. Thank you for letting me set the pace. I think it's different for us, after eight years of friendship in the platonic sense to just jump into bed right away. While I know we will get there, I think that it would do our relationship disservice to rush," she puts her hand on my knee.

"So, right now we could make out,"

"There can be some petting,"

"We both need to get some sleep and here you are talking about heavy petting," I lean my head back on the couch and groan.

"What do you mean we need to get some sleep? You're on summer break and I own my business, we could stay up all night if we wanted," Summer smiles.

"We could," I tilt my head.

She leans into me as my hand moves to cradle her head and pull her even closer to me. Our lips touch, our tongues run against one another, and after a moment of light kisses, the kiss deepens, and Summer has moved to sit astride my lap. Her fingertips thread through the back of my head as my hands run roughly up her back, pressing her into me.

She lightly moans into my mouth as her hips begin to move in circular motions. My hands move down to her hips and I hold on to her with my fingertips digging into her sides as she lowers herself fully onto my lap which leaves her thin shorts and my basketball shorts as the only clothing between our lower regions as she rubs against my rigid length.

My mind is exploding with thoughts. This is unfamiliar territory for us, and if she's just as nervous as I am, holy shit. She sucks on my tongue and then pulls back. Her skin is flushed, her eyes are dilated and heated with pure desire, and she is out of breath. Her hips are still moving in circular motions with my own, assisting her in feeling as much of me as possible. I'm biting my lower lip when her hands roam down my chest. She pulls my shirt over my head and discards it beside us on the couch as her hands trail across my chest.

"I know we need to stop this, but I just want a taste, just to get me through the night," she whispers as her fingertips trail my waist band. She bites her plump bottom lip and then slowly looks up to me in question.

FOURTEEN

Summer

I WANT to see more of him, to feel more of him. I know that we need to stop, but now I'm curious.

We should stop, but what's a little more. There's absolutely no harm in making out a little more.

My eyes look up to him for confirmation of a little more, but I see a slight hesitation and that makes me pull back.

"Everything okay?" I ask him.

"Yeah, everything is perfect right now," he nods.

"But?"

"How do you know there is a 'but'?" he asks.

"I can tell, spill it."

"If we continue this, we may go past that spot that you want to linger in, and I don't want you to get mad or regret anything that we do ever."

This is the Shaw that I could fall in love with. The considerate person, the guy who cares about the other person's feelings above his wants and desires.

I nod. "Thank you, but I know when to stop and right now, I honestly do not want to," I say after a moment of thought.

"What do you want, Summer?"

"I want you, Shaw. I've wanted you for maybe a long time, and I don't want to hold back on exploring this."

"What are you saying?" he asks, confirming one more time.

"If we're diving into a relationship, we dive into it head first. I want it all with you. I want the fast and the slow. I want to get carried away with you. I want the cautious and I want the reckless. I'm okay with whatever feels good, and this right here, really does."

His hands wrap around my waist and he stands up with my legs circling his hips.

"Where are we going?" I ask.

"Remember, there's a four-year-old sleeping in the house, I don't want him to come into the living room with you dry humping me." He says in between placing kisses along my neck and collarbone.

"So, instead he'll just walk into your room?" I laugh.

"No, that door will be locked, and you are free to dry hump me all you want with no worry of little eyes seeing anything."

We enter his bedroom and he locks the door with me still in his arms and then turns us around so he's sitting on the edge of his bed and I'm still sitting on top of him.

"I don't think I was aware of how strong you are before now," I admit, running my hands along his shoulders and down his biceps.

"Is that what you want to talk about right now? How strong I am?" he asks with a gleam in his eyes.

"We'll have to touch back on that subject later, because you've surely been hiding this body." I say before leaning back in and kissing him. I smile against the kiss, his hands move to the globes of my ass as my hips find a hardness in his pants and rub myself against it again.

My heart is quickening as I increase my movements. He nips at my shoulder as I grind myself on him. I hear his breathing getting labored while his hands grip tighter.

"Fuck, I don't think I've done this in a really long time," he says into my skin.

I lean back, slowing my hips, making sure that I catch his eyes to assure that he watches what I'm about to do.

I cross my arms over my chest to grab the hem of my tank top and begin to pull it up. I'm wearing a bra, but that doesn't stop this moment from being a defining moment in this thing between us. When I toss the shirt to the floor beside us, I reach behind my back and unsnap my bra to release. Shaw's eyes have gone wide and his mouth drops open. He licks his lips, looks up to me in silent question.

His hand moves slowly up to cup my breast as his head moves in. In slow-motion, I watch Shaw's tongue lash out and lick at my pebbled nipple. He sucks the tip into his mouth, causing tingling sensations to erupt in my body and my thighs to quiver. My breathing gets faster as he moves and repeats the same affection to my other breast. He watches my reaction as he pulls me flush against him. He kisses the valley between my breasts and trails up my chest to my neck and to my lips. The kiss is a slight jolt of lightning and I'm swept away under the current with him as he moves me so my back in against his comforter and he hovers over me.

He presses his hips into mine and I can feel his erection as he rubs it against me while he kisses me.

I moan lightly as the tip of his dick brushes against my sensitive body, wanting nothing more than to rid the rest of our clothes and to feel him against me.

My hands roam down the front of his body, across his

rippled abdomen, and to the trail of hair that leads inside his pants. My fingertips grip his waistband and I start to tug down. I get his shorts over his ass and now the only thing between us is my thin sleep shorts and his boxers.

One less layer is between us.

I can feel his dick pressing against my middle as our tongues dance together, our hips grind, and the skin of our chests rub against one another. My hands, with a mind of their own, reach again for the waistband of his boxers. I begin to pull down and Shaw's hand pauses me.

"Summer," he says low in warning.

"I want to feel you," I plead.

"Summer, we're moving really fast right now."

"I want to feel good," I say, "I want you to feel good."

"Babe, I'm feeling exceptional right now. Do you need a little more?" he asks while I nod.

He moves down my body and peppers kisses in a line down my body. When he gets to my waistband, he looks up. My breath has hitched at the possibility of what he's non-verbally asking, and I'm pretty sure that my heart is leaping out of my chest at this. I give a small nod and his fingers fit into the waistband and he drags down my shorts.

With an audible intake of his breath, I look down in worry.

"You aren't wearing any panties," he says quietly, staring at my pussy.

"No," I admit.

His fingertip traces over the landing strip across my pubic bone and down to where I can no longer see. I spread my legs as he situates himself in between them and just as his head lowers, the tip of his fingers run along my seam and I feel his tongue against me—there's a knock at his bedroom door.

"Daddy?" The small voice from the hallway calls out. "Daddy, your door is locked!"

FIFTEEN

Shaw

FUCK!
  Fuck!
  Fuck!

I'VE GOT one helluva erection, a beautiful naked woman on my bed, and I'm so very thankful that we moved this into the bedroom instead of continuing in the living room where this situation could have been a lot more awkward.

Summer's legs automatically close, with my head trapped still between them. She has some very powerful legs as it took a second for her to release for me to sit up fully.

With a sheepish look on her face, she mouths an apology and then begins to frantically look for her shirt. I pull her pants up quickly and search for my basketball shorts.

"Hold on buddy," I call out nearly falling head first onto the floor grabbing them from the other side of the bed. I lean over, chastely kiss Summer on the lips and then stand up. She pulls her shirt over her head and then lays in a fetal position on the bed to pretend that she is asleep—then I turn and answer the door.

"Why is your door locked, Daddy?" He asks while I block his from seeing inside the room.

"It's a habit buddy, I'm sorry. Everything good?"

"I wanted some milk, but my cup isn't on the counter and I can't reach the milk."

"Okay, let's go get some milk," I turn and do what I can to hide Summer in my room, but my son is quick and smart as a whip.

"Why is auntie Summer sleeping in your room?" he asks.

"What do you mean?" I ask.

"She wasn't in her room, and I saw her in your room," he points back towards the bedrooms.

"We were talking."

"With the door locked?" he asks.

"Mason, sometimes grown-ups need to talk about things privately."

"Oh, okay, Daddy."

I return to the bedroom and Summer is still in the position that I left her in. I turn off the light in my bedroom, hoping that she will stay and slide onto the bed beside her. I pull her closer to me and she shakes in laughter.

"That would have been so mortifying, if your door was unlocked and he walked in, while you were—you know," she turns on her back, throws her arm over her eyes and laughs.

"I would have just said that I was investigating for a tick," I quip.

"Why a tick?" she turns her head and asks in seriousness.

"Because last year, we went camping, you remember that weekend, well in preschool they were learning about bugs and he thought he had one on his butt, so I had to look. That would have been my automatic go to."

"Was it a tick?" She questions.

"No, it was a rock from the lake that was in his shorts." I say with a smile.

She laughs again.

I'm glad that this whole situation didn't make her run for her bedroom and hide away from me.

"I'm glad we moved from out there to in here, I mean he would have caught us with our pants down, no joke!" she laughs. I join in on the laughter and roll to my back as well. When the laughter dies down, I reach for her hand, intertwine our fingers together and put it on my stomach.

"I'm glad you didn't run," I finally say.

"I don't think that I would have been able to run far, I mean this is your house and all, you would know where to find me," she turns her head to face me.

"I know, but my son just interrupted me going down on you."

"Yeah, talk about a mood killer."

"We could totally revamp up that mood, if you want?" I lean up on my elbow and look down at her with a smile.

"While that would be great, because I've got a serious case of lady blue balls now, I think it's best if we just go to sleep."

"To be continued?" I ask with hope.

She reaches up and caresses my cheek with a happy smile. "To be continued."

I HAD to get Mason back to his mother's house by ten in the morning, and with the flurry of the morning, I only caught glimpses of Summer while she was moving to and from rooms getting ready for her morning. She had planned a later start time but woke up this morning later than she usually did in a rush.

I keep myself busy getting a curriculum ready for the summer session of adult GED classes that I teach at the local community college in the middle of the summer to help stay busy during the summer. The curriculum is the same, but I like to revamp it every so often, to assure that I keep with current events and learning tools.

Teaching adults wasn't as fun as it was teaching children, it lacked creativity, but I enjoyed the feeling that I was helping someone succeed in one of their goals, or helping them advance when before, for whatever reason, they couldn't finish high school.

My cell notifications were dinging, one notification after another. I grab my phone and see Summer is texting. I pull the messages up and scroll up to start at the beginning.

Summer: No Mason tonight, right?

Summer: I was thinking, maybe we can have a date

Summer: With a special desert

Summer: That means we can start something that may have begun last night.

Summer: Or not. Up to you.

I laugh at the nervousness in her texts and lean back in my chair, ready to make her blush and play a different game.

Me: I think what I want to do is skip dinner and go straight to desert.

Me: You know, I would strip you from your clothes again, lay you out on my bed, and lick your pretty pussy until you were squirming beneath me

Me: and then...

I wait and let that linger for her, just in case she wasn't able to see the texts right away. Immediately, I see the thought bubble come up on the screen.

Summer: And then?

I smile, knowing that I have her curiosity peaked.

Me: And then we'll see. The options are limitless.

Summer: You're the devil. I'm off at six

Me: I'll CU then

She doesn't respond and I use the time between now and when she's off of work to go grocery shopping. While I'm not an amazing chef, I should make sure that I have the staples in the house since Summer lives here now.

Lives here.

Summer lives here, in my house.

Wow. I never thought that would be such a strong phrase to think, but it is. The thought alone feels like a normal thought, something that has always been. But I know that just a few months ago, she was living with douchebag Colin, thinking that everything was fine. And now, she's here with me. Am I the rebound? Is that what this is?

Surely no, we wouldn't risk our friendship on a rebound which might ruin the friendship. Instead, we're starting something completely new from scratch. It's developing organically, not forced. If you don't count Sloane meddling with that whole kiss thing after the BBQ.

Right?

SIXTEEN

Summer

"SO, hooker-face, you've been dodging my phone calls now for a few days. What the hell?" Sloane says throwing a paperback on the cash counter.

"Are you buying this?" I ask her with a quirked eyebrow.

"I will if it's any good?"

"It is, but it's book one of three. You may just want to buy all three now, so you can properly binge read."

"But then I won't have an excuse to come and visit my bestie," Sloane pouts.

"Bullshit, you always have excuses."

"That's true. Anyway, so that kiss the other night, that was pretty hot."

"What kiss?" I play dumb and ask.

"You know, with the hot guy that you're living with."

"Oh yeah, that one. Yeah, it was a good kiss."

"And?" she pries.

"And what?"

"And has anything else happened?" she asks, leaning in.

I look away and can feel my face flush. With a smile on my face, I ring up the book for her. "That will be ten dollars and nine cents." I say to her, avoiding her gaze.

"Why are you beet red and not looking me in the eye?" she asks knowingly.

"No reason," I reply.

"You guys have kissed since then, haven't you?" she says.

"I don't know what you're talking about," I say as the door rings open.

"Hey Sum? I need some help." Shaw calls out walking into view. "Oh shit, hey Sloane."

"Maybe you can answer my questions, since this one lit up like Rudolph's nose, what's going on between you two?" Sloane turns and points at him.

He holds his hands up in front of him and looks quickly to me. I shrug and smile, happy now that the pressure is all on him and off of me.

"What?" he asks, milking more time as he walks closer.

"How was that kiss from the BBQ?" Sloane asks.

"Oh that, yeah it was good," he replies coming to stand by me. "I need some help; I don't shop for food and what do you eat regularly?"

"Why are you buying her food?" Sloane looks suspiciously between us.

"Because she lives with me, and people need to eat food to keep living or something," Shaw says matter-of-factly.

"Have you guys kissed again?" Sloane asks.

"I'll eat anything, fruits, veggies, meats." I reply, ignoring Sloane.

"No special weird gluten-free type things?" he asks.

"Nope," I smile at him.

"Okay, good."

"You guys! Quit ignoring me!" Sloane huffs out as Shaw steps into me, wraps his hand around my waist and pulls me to him. With my hand on his chest, he leans in, rubs his nose against mine and then kisses me so passionately that it's almost like he should dip me. When he pulls back, he smiles, chastely kisses me again and pulls away.

"I'll see you later at home, see ya later Sloane." He shouts and waves as he exits the bookstore.

Sloane's mouth is hanging open, her eyes are wide with her hands posted on her hips.

"Well then," she says after a moment of complete silence. "I guess that answers that, you hussy."

"Answers what?" I ask her.

"You two, playing house, sucking faces and shit."

"So crass, so come on, you owe me ten dollars and nine cents, pay up lady!"

"Were you planning on hiding that?" Sloane asks, digging in her purse.

"Hiding what?" I say.

"Stop it with the games, you two are bumping uglies."

"No uglies have been bumped," I defend.

"Ok, bumping pretties, although imagining a penis, that's not pretty and accompanied by two wrinkly hairy balls. No thanks, bumping uglies it is. I just can't." She shakes her head with a disgusted look on her face.

"I think a penis is actually quite nice. I like how they look," I say.

"You would. You're too all up in a new penis, so of course it looks more fascinating than the standard penis."

"I haven't seen Shaw's penis; I'm talking penises in general. They fascinate me. Sometimes, it looks like they're smiling."

"Of course, they are, they're about to throw up if someone

plays with it and makes it happy," Sloane motions like she's giving a hand job.

"This is one conversation that shouldn't be had in public," I say looking around.

"Aren't you glad you don't have one of those smart home devices in here, I mean imagine us talking about penises and Alexa listening in and sending all that conversation to NASA."

"NASA? Why would it go to NASA?" I ask.

"Because they listen to our conversations."

"Um, no they don't," I shake my head.

"There was that whole Wiki-something a few years ago, when that one Snow-man guy leaked a bunch of information and said that NASA is always listening, don't you remember that?" Sloane asks.

"And you call yourself a teacher, Sloane, that was the NSA, not NASA."

"Wait, what?"

"NSA is national security, whereas NASA is space," I explain.

Sloane has embarrassment written all over her face, "You know, sometimes all these acronyms are just jumbled up and I say things that I didn't mean to say."

"Now that this lesson is over, can we go to a new subject? I would rather not be talking about penises when customers come in," I ask her.

"Okay, okay. So, this thing with Shaw, what?" she asks.

"We're seeing where it all takes us."

"I can tell, but what the heck happened after Luke and I left? Shaw was quite adamant on us leaving. He called for an Uber, then pushed us both out of the house. Were you guys getting it on like right after we left?" She asks.

"I mean, we weren't really getting it on. We talked and then we kissed again. But we didn't hook up or anything really, a little last night, but we were interrupted, which kind of hampered the mood a bit." I say blushing.

"Interrupted?" she questions.

"Mason was home last night, it was the night in the week that he stays at Shaw's, but it was late, and I was all romanticized from the bath and wine."

"Wait, back up a second here. A bath? Wine? You are leaving some key points out of this story."

"I had a shit day yesterday, when I got home late last night after closing, he was awake, and he drew me a bath and had a bottle of wine waiting for me. There were candles and everything, so I had a few glasses of wine, then he was passed out on the couch when I finished. When I woke up, he was still sleepy, he woke up and we ended up in his room."

"And then you got interrupted?"

"Yes," I nod. "He was just about to dine downtown when Mason knocked on the bedroom door," I reply blushing.

"Holy shit, you were caught with your pants down?"

"We had the door locked, but yes."

Well, so was any of the talk that Shaw had coming in here code for continuing to dine downtown, or was that really about food?

"It was about food, you perv."

But that's not to say that the texts earlier weren't about continuing last night.

SEVENTEEN

Shaw

The house is quiet and for the first time in a long time, I'm nervous.

I haven't had a significant date in quite some time, and this one is important.

It's Summer.

It's Summer and me.

On a date, well I mean, I cooked dinner for her as a date.

Shit, should I have taken her out for dinner?

Now, I'm standing over my salad spinner, worrying about whether or not my plans for the evening were right.

All thoughts are erased as soon as I heard the front door open, then close. She walks through the house and sets her bag on the chair by the table.

She sniffs the air and smiles. "It smells nice in here, I thought you didn't know how to cook?"

"I can cook things, whether or not they taste good is a different story."

"Good point, so sir, what are you making for dinner?" She asks, standing beside me and looking into the spinner.

"Salad, garlic bread and Mostaccioli." I smile proudly.

"Is this the recipe from your mom?" She asks excitedly.

"Sure is," I nod.

"Yes!" she says excitedly.

"You remember it?" I ask her surprised.

"Oh, hell yeah. Why do you think that whenever I went to your parents with you, that was something that they made?"

"Because, it's easy to make a lot of?"

"Your mom would call me and ask me what I wanted, my answer was always this."

"So, what you're telling me is that I did good with dinner?" I ask hopeful.

"We'll see how it turns out," she winks and walks away. I reach out for her and grab her to pull her back over to me.

"Hey," I say.

"Hey," she replies.

"Good day?"

"After Sloane grilled me, yes."

"Grilled you?"

"Well, we had quite a comical conversation and then we talked about you and me a little. That PDA that you did was perfect, she was probably spinning situations in her mind and then you come in and light it up for her."

"I should have grabbed your boob too, huh?"

"No, that would have been entirely inappropriate," Summer says with a straight face.

"Well in that case, I'll keep all boob gropes private," I say, "go change, dinner is ready in ten."

Summer leaves the room and returns shortly wearing a sundress with her hair up. I groan silently as I look at how short the skirt is and adjust myself behind the counter.

"Wine?" I ask her.

She nods and I fill up a glass for her. We eat dinner together and make small talk about our day. We unwind from dinner on the couch and I hand her the remote.

"What?" She asks.

"You choose," I say.

"The man hands the woman the remote, mark this moment down in history," she giggles.

"I'm not sure that's what is happening. I think I'm just letting you choose what we watch."

"I want to watch," she looks to the ceiling in thought and then has a devilish grin, "the bachelorette."

"Why do people watch that stuff?" I ask, groaning, regretting the decision to let her choose.

"Guilty pleasures. I think ultimately, we all want to live in that kind of fairytale."

"Please educate me on how going on a reality show is like a fairytale?"

"Dating sucks. Meeting someone is hard, the show helps with that, and then you have catfights, so you feel wanted, even though it's pathetic and at the end you have a lot of kisses under your belt, three potential hook-ups and a potential life partner." She shrugs.

"You say that as if these couples actually end up together."

"Some do, some try, and some don't. I think it's ultimately up to what happens once the tape stops rolling that decides it."

"And if you and I were in a reality show, what would it be called?" I ask on a whim.

"Hmmm. I imagine it would be something like Survivor."

"What? That's just weird."

"You put me on the spot, I don't think you and I would be any of these specific shows, but I can see it being something that tests your skills. I think that is what we do for one another, we test, and we solve."

"That's the weirdest analogy to dating," I say.

"Is that what we're doing?" She asks quietly.

"Dating? I mean, sure. Or we're at least trying to figure out how to define what this is. I like you, and you like me. We're best of friends, and we're going into a whole new facet of our relationship. I think it's dating." I reply.

"Okay," she says, leaning her head back.

"Would you call it something different?" I ask her, pulling her against me with her hand settling on my thigh.

"I think if we wanted to define it, that would be how I would. So, does this make you my boyfriend?"

"Do you want me to be your boyfriend?"

"The last boyfriend that I had, ultimately cheated on me, so I kinda have an aversion to the title right now."

"Partner, I'm your partner. How is that?"

"I like that."

"Can I ask you a question?" I start. "This new partnership, this dating one another, are you ready for that, or is this something to get over Colin?" I take a deep breath.

She pulls away from me, faces me and grabs my hand. "Shaw, I would never use you as a rebound. You are too important to me to be something to toss away."

"I just, Summer, I just, this thing is something that I've thought about over the years. The 'what ifs' about you and me. And I just don't want to be a fleeting moment in your timeline."

"You will never be a fleeting moment, or something that is not monumental. I mean it, you can trust me with this. I've thought a lot about what this means between us and I don't think that either of us would be careless with one another in that capacity."

"Monumental, eh?" I say with a smile.

"Were you just fishing for a compliment?" She asks.

"Not at all, but it's a bonus that I got one out of the conversation that's been weighing on my mind."

EIGHTEEN

WITH MASON at his moms Shaw and I have free rein of the entire house. We started watching a show that developed into little caressing here and there. It became apparent when Shaw began massaging my shoulders, then kissing my neck that he wasn't interested in the show and therefore he turned the game around on me and I ended up straddling his lap again.

Then when kissing became pretty hot, he slid down onto the floor and lifted my skirt.

Which is where he is now. My legs are open and he's kissing the inside of my thigh, making his way to the center of my body. I feel the tip of his finger breach my entrance and my body rises from the couch cushion. Shaw's available hand wraps around my hip and pulls me down and into his mouth. His tongue lashes out and I feel the tip of his tongue lick up and down my seam.

I'm panting already as my fingers thread through his hair and I push him into me.

He hums against me as he moves his finger in and out of me, adding another as my hips move with him accordingly. I moan lightly as his tongue finds my clit, and he lightly flicks my pleasure nub.

I'm almost grinding my hips against his face when I hear the damn phone ringing from the coffee table in front of us. We ignore the phone as he fucks me with his tongue and his finger, bringing me to the cusp of an orgasm and then pulling back to torture me further. He uses his fingers and hooks them inside as he blows on my clit.

When I moan loudly and push his head back to where I want him, the phone rings again. I groan and throw darts at the interruption with my eyes, but Shaw continues on his mission. The phone goes silent again, just as Shaw takes the tiny bud of joy into his mouth and sucks. His fingers are moving in and out of me and suddenly my orgasm is right there. My legs straighten, my back arches, and I grab Shaw's head and yell his name into the quietness of the living room. A moment later, I can feel my legs and can breathe again, when the phone rings for a third time.

Shaw sits up straight and in quickness he grabs the phone. "What?" he answers in a brash tone, the look on his face in pure annoyance.

"Shit, okay. We'll be right there, okay. Yeah," he hangs up and looks at me. "We need to go." He stands up and holds his hand out to me.

"What's happening?" I ask.

"Mason is in the emergency room, some kind of allergic reaction."

"Okay. I'll go um, change and you need to go wash you face," I tell him as he grabs his keys, adjusts himself and put his shoes on.

"What? Why?" he asks confused.

"Because I just came on your face."

HAND IN HAND, Shaw and I are rushing into the emergency room up to the information desk.

"My son, Mason Renner was brought in with an allergic reaction, I'm here to see him?" Shaw rushes out.

"I'm sorry. His father is already in the room with him and his mother. Only two visitors at a time, and they are required to be family, sir."

"I am the father!" Shaw seethes through a clenched jaw.

"I got this, calm down, getting angry at her won't help," I squeeze his hand. "Excuse me, you see the gentlemen who went in with Marie, Mason's mother is her boyfriend. This is Shaw Renner, his biological and only father." I turn back to Shaw, "give me your ID?" I show the ID to the nurse and she nods.

"I apologize for the confusion sir, the mother indicated that they were both the parents. We will see that you are able to go back. Would your wife like a visitor badge as well?"

"Oh, I'm—"

"Yes, please." Shaw says squeezing my hand.

We're sitting, waiting to go back into the room. He's nervously clutching onto my hand and my knee is bouncing in anticipation. A moment later Marie and her boyfriend come out of the hallway and lock eyes on us. She walks over to us, just as we stand. Her eyes watch us stand and zero in on our joined hands, then she looks at us both.

"What happened? Where is my son?" Shaw asks.

"Mr. and Mrs. Renner, you are free to go into the room now," the nurse said.

"Mr. and Mrs. Renner?" Marie asks with a sour look on her face.

"She's assuming," Shaw says. "Marie, what happened?"

"I'd like the know the same," she narrows her gaze again on our hands.

"Marie, this is not the time or place for jealousy. Our son is in the hospital. What the fuck happened?" Shaw asks.

"He ate some nutrition bar and he had a reaction; they've shot him with an epi-pen and he's resting now."

"What kind of bar?" I ask as Marie cuts an annoyed gaze at me.

When Marie doesn't acknowledge my question, Shaw pushes past her and we move to the front desk. Shaw leans in and asks for the room number, then he's leading me through the hall to the room. We stand in the doorway and look in on Mason. His tiny frame in the large hospital bed, an IV beside his bed and he's got a pinched expression on his face.

Shaw steps forward, and I pull my hand out of his grasp finally. Shaw stops and looks back confused.

"I'm right here, I'll be here and won't go anywhere," I say quietly.

"I want you by my side," he replies holding out his hand.

"Are you sure?" I ask.

"Summer, my little boy is laying in a hospital bed, I need you. I need my best friend."

I can't deny him that. I slip my hand back in his and we sit beside Mason's bed. I'm leaning on Shaw's shoulder when I hear Mason say something.

"Daddy?" His voice is groggy.

"Hey buddy," Shaw and I immediately stand up.

"Auntie Summer," Mason's eyes dart to me and he smiles.

"Hey little guy, how you are doing?" I ask him.

"It hurt to breathe, and lumps were all over me," Mason says quietly.

"How do you feel now?" Shaw asks.

"Sleepy," Mason closes his eyes for a moment.

"I'll go get Marie, she may want to see him," I say.

"Ignore her rudeness, don't let anything that she says to you affect you," he says cupping my face and pulling me in for a quick kiss.

I smile, squeeze his hand and lean in to give Mason a quick kiss as he opens his eyes.

"Where are you going?" He asks.

"I'm going to go get your mommy, I'll be back soon."

I find my way out of the winding halls of the hospital and into the waiting room to Marie and her boyfriend sitting. Marie stands with an annoyed posture as I approach.

"Mason is awake, I came back out, so you can go in," I say as politely as I can.

"How nice of you to let me go and see my son, Summer." She says with obvious annoyance and then looks back at her boyfriend. "Are you coming?"

"No, only two people at a time. I'm fine. I'll hang out, grab something for us to eat." He stands and walks away.

Marie gives me a once over and rolls his eyes. "I always knew it," she says and walks away.

Always knew what?

NINETEEN

THE TENSION in the room is high whenever Marie is in it. While she and I had a rocky relationship, that doesn't negate the fact that we shared a great kid. Mason is awake and the doctor is giving him a skin test based off of the ingredients from the food that he ate, which lead to the hospital visit.

We haven't noticed any other allergic reactions before, but the kid is also a picky eater, so his palate is quite bland.

There were reactions to about four different types of nuts, with hazelnuts and cashews being the worst reactions for the tests.

We are given epi-pens for both households and after ten hours at the hospital, Mason is released and everyone is exhausted.

Marie's attitude didn't lessen all day, especially once Mason was awake.

Summer and I hug Mason and we both told him that we loved him as we left. I am exhausted and so is she. Most of her night, she spent sitting in the waiting room and I felt horrible that she couldn't be with me and Mason.

"I'm sorry that our date was cut short unexpectedly," I say.

"I think there was a good reason, so it's okay. How are you doing?" she asks.

"I'm tired and annoyed. I'm sorry for how Marie was, but I am really glad you were there."

"I'm glad I was there too," she says, rolling her head toward me.

"Did Marie say anything to you?" I ask after a beat.

"She said something like she always knew, but I'm not sure what that meant."

"Always knew?" I look at her when I stop at the light.

"Yeah, she didn't say anything else though, so I'm not sure it's really that big of a deal."

"Weird. She sure as shit didn't like that the nurse called you Mrs. Renner. I kinda liked it," I wink at her.

"Don't get too ahead of yourself there buddy, I'm not sure if I really like you or not."

"Oh, trust me. You like me. I can tell."

"Oh yeah, and suddenly you know everything?"

"Men always know all the things."

"Except directions, how to find things and how to make decisions."

"Ouch."

DESPITE THE NIGHT ending in exhaustion, I still feel like the date before the hospital was going really well. When we returned to the house, I kissed her at her bedroom door and then went to my bedroom.

My body is exhausted, but my mind is running a mile a

minute. A light tap on my door startles me and also excites me as I know who is on the other end of the door. I lean up on my elbows and tell her to come in.

Summer pokes her head in and smiles, "I can't sleep," she whispers.

I move from the center of my bed to allow space for her and pat the space beside me. She comes in and settles in beside me. My arm goes around her and she leans her cheek on my chest.

"Tonight was... interesting," she says.

"Tell about it, I'm sorry again that our date got interrupted."

"Stop apologizing for that. When there are other responsibilities in one's life, sometimes those kinds of things take precedence. I love Mason, and I know that he means the world to you," she says.

"I just don't want you to feel like you aren't important too, because Summer, you are very important to me," I reply.

"Your son will always come first, I know that."

"While in some ways, that's true. I think that in other ways we would as well. I want to have a relationship that I can show my son is strong, I want to set an example for that. I want him to be in a loving home, and to see what it's like to love someone for real, it's kinda like I'd be setting him up to be an amazing adult."

"Mason has you as a dad, I think that's a good start," she puts her chin on me and looks up at me.

"Summer?" I begin.

"Yeah, Shaw?"

"Thank you so much for being so strong for me tonight, I don't think I allowed myself to really feel what was happening, but you holding my hand, and sticking up for me to that nurse may have seemed insignificant to you, but to me—well, just thank you."

"Shaw, even if we were still just friends, I would have done the same."

"I know, I don't know why, but it seems like maybe now that we're taking this a level further, that it's different, it takes on a whole different meaning, even though, it doesn't."

"We should quit trying to analyze this," she whispers.

"I agree."

"Shaw?" she says resting her cheek on my chest again. "Thank you for making sure that I was included tonight."

I WAKE up in the morning in the same position that I fell asleep, with Summer in my arms, and my arms around her. Except for her being beside me, half of her body is on top of mine and my cock is very aware of it. I look down and her hand is extremely close to the tent in my boxers that if I was to take a deep breath, her hand would come into contact with me and I'm not entirely sure that I could handle that.

When I went down on her last night, I came in my pants and I was somewhat happy that the emergency came up and saved me from that embarrassment. When I went to wash my face and hands, I changed my boxers and it was almost as if it never happened.

Summer hums and stretches out, her hand brushing over the crown of my erection, causing me to hiss and jolt at the sensation of her touch. She opens her eyes and I assume that she sees what her hand came into contact with. She slowly moves her hand to my groin and with the tip of her finger, she traces the tip.

"Good morning to you," she says continuing to trace an invisible line along my straining erection. She turns her head up to me and smiles, "is this a normal occurrence?"

"I feel like that's a trick question," I reply.

She sits up and stares at my groin, then looks back to me. "Shaw?"

"Yeah, Summer?" I say, unsure of where this conversation will be going.

"I want to try something," she says, "do you trust me?"

"You know that I do," I reply immediately.

She sits up and pulls off her tank top and slides her short shorts down her long tan legs. She's wearing a purple thong and my mouth goes dry. Her breasts bounce from the movement of removing her shirt and then she turns and sits on my lap facing me. My cock is right in front of her pussy. I reach up and palm one of her breasts and then she reaches down and pulls my cock out of the boxers through the hole in the front. She gives my cock three strokes and licks her lips as she watches her hand.

This is the first time that she's seeing me in the flesh and the way she's looking at my cock, touching me and licking her lips, is making me harder than I thought possible. She slides her panties to the side and takes my cock and fits it between her lips. She moves up and down, her wetness coating my shaft as a loud animalistic groan reverberates through the room.

My hands fly to her hips and I hold on to her while she languidly moves on top of me. The sounds of skin against skin sliding and her tiny breaths are all that I can hear and it's taking every ounce of my will to not take my cock and thrust into her.

Except this is her leading this moment, and I'm not about to fuck it up when it feels so fucking good with what she's doing. If all goes to well, there's plenty of time for everything to happen and for the rest of our lives.

The rest of our lives.

Yes, I can get behind that.

My best friend, as my partner in life.

Yes, that has quite the ring to it.

TWENTY

Summer

I MOAN LOUDLY as I have his dick angled perfectly against my sex to hit my clit on each movement of my hips. I look down at Shaw, and it's as if he's lost in this moment as much as I am. His eyes aren't focused, but I can tell that he's into this.

I wonder what would happen if I shifted a little higher and slip him inside. We could play just the tip and that could be an easy ice-breaker into sex for us.

Even though, with him pleasuring me to an intense orgasm last night and this right now, I'm pretty sure we're deep into the physical levels of a relationship between two people.

Curiosity takes over and I go an extra step and move up on my knees higher to with the downstroke, Shaw's dick in my hand breaches my entrance instead of glides against it. I move quickly, playing with inserting just the crown of his dick, that makes his groans get louder and then suddenly, he grips my hips stopping me from making any more moves.

"Sum," he warns, "this is skirting the edge of danger."

"Do you want me to stop?" I ask him in a breathy sigh. His dick is nudging against my entrance and I can feel the warmth of him.

"That's a really hard questions for me to answer right now," he admits.

"Do you have a condom?" I ask.

"Are you sure?" He asks me.

"Do you have a condom, Shaw?"

He releases his hold on me, and I don't move as he reaches into the table beside his bed and grabs the strip of condoms in the shiny gold foil. He tears one off and holds it up.

"Is this what you want?" he asks.

"Yes," I whisper.

"Put it on me then," he directs.

I take it from him with trembling hands and lean back on his thighs. He leans up and his hand snakes between my legs. He slips a finger into me as he pulls my breast into his mouth.

"Shaw, you're distracting me from the job at hand," I sigh as his finger plunges all the way into me.

"Does this feel good to you, Summer?"

"Yes," I hiss out.

"I want to learn everything that you like. I want to kiss every piece of you, and I want your moans to be mine."

He plunges in and out of me with slow workings of his wrist and finally, he's sheathed, and I look at him.

"I want you," I whisper.

"You have me, you've always had me."

I move back, hovering over his dick and look to him.

"Put me inside you," he tells me.

Both of us watch his dick disappear into my body and once he's buried to the hilt, I throw my head back and finally breath out the breath I was holding. Shaw's jaw is clenched, and I pulse my muscles encasing his dick and watch him.

"I need a moment to get used to being so full," I tell him.

"Take all the time that you need, baby. I think I need that too."

After a minute of silence, I begin to move my hips up and down, his dick fitting perfectly inside me and despite the condom, I can feel all of him in the most delicious way.

Shaw massages my breasts and pumps his hips from underneath, meeting my hips with each demand. He takes my nipple into his mouth and sucks while growling in satisfaction.

I have all the control right now, but I want him to take me. I want him to show me just how much he's wanted this. I pull his face to mine and kiss him. I kiss him so passionately, that I'm lost in the kiss and don't even realize that Shaw's hands have wrapped around my middle and I'm being moved. I'm on my back in an instant without breaking contact with Shaw and he's hovering over me.

"I know this is the first time between us, but I don't know if I will be able to control myself any more than I already have," he says against my throat as his hips pump slowly into me.

"I need you; I'll take whatever you give me, just make me come?" I plead.

"With absolute pleasure," he takes my lips and sears them with a passionate kiss before moving up to his forearms and holding his weight off of me. "Are you ready?"

I manage a nod, and within a split second, Shaw pulls out almost entirely and then thrusts into me repeatedly. He's so deep into me, that I swear that I can feel him in my throat. I arch my neck as he pounds into me, taking his dick almost entirely out and filling me so perfectly as he nips at the delicate skin of my neck. I feel my orgasm building with each thrust, with my fingertips digging into his sides.

"Shaw! Shaw! I'm– I'm– I'm—"

"I'm right there, baby! Fuck, you feel so damn good!" He expels.

I don't bother announcing when my body turns into jelly, I can feel my inner walls clenching his dick as he pumps faster into me releasing himself in the condom. Lights are erupting behind my eyelids, a silent scream is coming from my open mouth and my toes curl in delight.

It takes a moment to come back to reality and when I do, Shaw is peppering kisses along my chest, shoulders and neck while his hips languidly pump into me. My hands move and I push my fingers through his hair and pull him to kiss my lips.

He takes my mouth and I feel the amount of care, passion, and love that he spills into the kiss. It almost scares me, but at the same time, I know that in this moment, I'm truly in love with my best friend and that changing our friendship into a relationship was one of the best decisions that we've ever made.

TWENTY-ONE

SHAW

BASKING in the newness of a relationship that has taken it to the next level was short lived. While I would have loved to be wrapped up in bed naked with Summer for the rest of the day, she had a business to run and I had a site visit for my summer GED classroom and a meeting with one of the administrators.

We showered together, and as soon as I made sure that Summer was properly cleaned, I dirtied her up again for the excuse that I missed a spot, so I should just start all over again. I made her come twice in the shower and I know and now I was sure that I knew what pure happiness was.

There was no awkwardness from the morning after that I can tell and from our interactions from this morning, we're the best we've ever been.

After a boring day, I just wanted Summer to come back and for us to go back into our cocoon, except she was closing the store tonight and I was properly worn out.

I was asleep on the couch with the television on when

Summer came home from her day. She didn't wake me, but covered me with a blanket and retreated to her room. I woke up in the middle of the night to a dark house, rolled off the couch, then stumbled down the hallway. I walked past the open door to the room that Summer was staying in, to it being empty. I took the few extra steps to my bedroom and was relieved that there, in the center of my bed, laid Summer. She hugged my pillow to her and took up more than half of the bed, but I was happy to see her here rather than in the other room. When we were both fully awake, we would need to talk about what this relationship now means for the official sleeping arrangements of the house, but for right now, I pulled off my sweats and shirt to climb in beside her. Slowly, I replaced my pillow with my body and as she snuggled into me; I smiled at the feeling of how this whole relationship has made me feel.

THE EARLY MORNING light shone in from the blinds and my bed is missing a beautiful brunette who was here when I came to bed last night. I slowly move to a sitting position and grab my shirt off the floor. I step into my sweatpants and go in search of Summer.

She isn't anywhere in the house and when I peek out the front door, her car isn't in the driveway beside my own. I wander through the house in confusion.

It isn't time for the bookstore to open, and I don't see any notes anywhere that I can see. I run my hand through my hair, and retreat back to my bedroom to grab my towels to start on my day.

I come out of the shower to find Summer sitting on my bed looking contemplative and staring at the blank wall across from where she's sitting.

"What's wrong?" I ask her.

"Huh?" she looks up in confusion.

"Is everything okay? You weren't around when I woke up," I ask her, sitting down beside her in my towel.

"I went for a jog," she says simply.

"A jog? You don't run."

"Okay, so I went for a walk. I woke up and couldn't fall back asleep, so I went for a walk," she says with a roll of her eyes. "You know me too well."

"A walk. Is this because of what happened last night?" I ask.

"No. Yes. No. I'm happy. It's nothing about you and me. That's all alright. I just had a lot on my mind and I thought that walking would clear it right up."

Unsure of where she's going, I decide to see if she will confide in me a little more.

"What's on your mind?" I ask.

"You remember my staff who never showed up and I had to go back to the store that one night?"

I nod.

"Well, if you've noticed, I've been working a little more. She still hasn't returned any phone calls, so I've been trying to brainstorm what my next move is. I obviously need to hire someone else, or I'm going to spread myself too thin."

"So, you went on a walk?" I say in a question.

"I hoped that it would get my blood pumping, in turn get my mind moving and coming up with a plan. You know that if I'm in planning mode, I need to be moving," she says.

"Figure any of it out?"

"Not a single bit. All I know is that I will need to hire someone in place of her and will need to work more until then."

"I can call my mom, you know she loves books and would be a helpful person to do some stuff in the shop."

She looks at me, her eyes warming, and takes an audible breath while running her hand through her messy hair.

"Do you think she has the time?" she asks.

"Of course, she's retired," I shrug, pulling out my phone.

"True, but she's the busiest retired woman that I've ever known. Have you seen her calendar?"

I shake my head. I know my parents are always going out of town on those day tripper bus trips, but I never really paid much attention. Mason spends at least one afternoon a weekend with her, but she doesn't really talk to me much about any of the other stuff she is doing.

"How do you know how busy she is?" I ask.

"She comes by the shop regularly and gives me the latest run down," she replies simply.

"Oh, she does? Has she been in recently?" I quirk an eyebrow with a mischievous smile, then hold up my hand as I place the phone to my ear, knowing it's one of her pet peeves to ask a question and then hold off on allowing her to answer. Summer shakes her head in answer, but of course I can see that she wants to say more.

"Hello?" my mother answers the phone loudly.

"Ma? You busy?" I ask.

"I'm never busy for my loving and only son."

"Good," I pull the phone away from my ear, set it on speaker phone and then put it on the counter between Summer and myself. "Do you have any interest on doing some volunteer work?"

"Oh honey, I don't think I have the energy for a classroom full of six and seven year old's anymore."

"Oh, no. Not with my class, although I would love for you to come and read to them like usual next semester, but I'm calling on behalf of my girlfriend."

Summer waves her hand and mouths something to me, but

since I'm trying to not laugh and to push her hands out of the way, I can't tell what she's saying.

"Since when do you have a girlfriend and why is this the first that I'm hearing of this? I think it would be smart of me to meet this mystery woman if you're asking me to volunteer with someone. I mean really, Shaw. I don't think that's a good way to introduce a woman to your mother." I can tell by the unpleased tone of her voice that she's disappointed. Before she can continue to think poorly of me, I laugh.

"Mom, you already know her."

"I do?"

"Yes, you've known her for a while, in fact—"

"Shaw, stop being a jerk. Hello Janet," Summer chimes in as she swats at my shoulder.

"Summer? Dear? Is that you?" she asks.

"Yes, it's me. Shaw's being mean, ignore him."

"I do, most of the time. But why is he getting an old woman's hopes up that he's got a woman and fallen in love? Such cruel behavior, if you ask me," I hear more disappointment in her tone.

"Well, you see, he wasn't really lying," Summer says slowly.

"You can't be saying that you two are together? That's the funniest thing that I've ever heard, you're too smart for him, dear."

"Hey! I resent that. I'm smart too, mom!" I defend myself.

"Enough with the jokes already," my mother says.

"It's not a joke, mom."

TWENTY-TWO

Summer

I WASN'T PLANNING on announcing the relationship to his mom like this.

Hell. I didn't really even think that was something done much anymore. I never met Colin's parents, and relationships just sorta happen when you are an adult.

I shake my head and take in a deep breath.

"Well, you see, we really haven't had *the* conversation about a relationship status or anything and my Facebook still says 'single', but we're traversing through the waters," I say leaning over the phone.

"She's lying. We're full blown dating. We even already live together." Shaw says with a smirk.

"Only because I needed a place to stay!" I say to him through clenched teeth.

"So then, that's the truth." He pushes back.

"You're so annoying sometimes," I shake my head.

"Is this a new lover's spat? Kids, kids, can we get to the point of the call. You need a volunteer, Summer dear?"

"Sorry, yes. I have a missing staff member and can only spread myself so thin."

"You know how much I love your store, how often do you need me, I will need to make sure it doesn't interfere with any other obligations,"

"See, I told you she was busy!" I say to Shaw, who rolls his eyes. "Whenever you have the free time, really, you would be doing me a favor."

Janet and I figure out a schedule for the next few days and I smile, feeling instantly lighter.

"Now, about the matter of you two dating..." she says changing the subject.

MASON IS due over to the house for the weekend tonight and I'm nervous about how Shaw and I will act around him. We discussed after speaking with his mom this morning how to go about presenting the news to Mason, but I was still strong on the belief that it should happen organically. But after more discussion on not wanting to keep secrets, we decided that why not spread the news more?

We've already come out to a few friends and Shaw's mother, so it's not a huge secret. We've passed the point of no return, as we've slept with one another, so even if the relationship was short lived, something has changed and it's pretty apparent.

Unless Shaw has always looked at me like he wants to forgo dinner and eat me instead, I'm not sure if we will be able to curtail everything that happens between us.

Having a conversation with a four-year-old is easy, but all day while at the shop, my stomach was doing flips and I wasn't sure which end was up.

"Hey boss, I know that Tasha hasn't called in, so if you need me to work more hours, since it's summer, I totally can," Becky offers.

"Thanks Beck, I have a volunteer coming in, but I think I can rework some of the schedule to accommodate. If you want to write up your ideal schedule, I'll see what I can do." I say with a smile.

"You're the best. I'll make sure to have it here for you tomorrow. Anything that I need to know?" she asks.

I run down the day's events and then give her the information for the weekly book club that comes in on Fridays and then leave to go home.

Go home.

Home is currently with the guy that I'm dating.

The guy who I've been just friends with for most of my adult life.

The guy who I've recently only opened my eyes to.

The guy who I'm falling fiercely in love with so quickly in a different capacity than I have previously.

SHAW COOKED spaghetti and left me a warm plate to eat upon returning to the house. Shaw gave Mason his shower and then we settled on the couch to hang out and watch a show before Mason went to bed. He sat between us, snuggled into my side as he normally does when we're on a couch together.

My hand rested on his shoulder, my thumb lightly moving along his soft skin.

Shaw holds up the remote, mutes the cartoon, and turns his body to us.

"Hey buddy, can we talk to you for a minute?" Shaw starts.

Oh crap, okay, we're doing this now. My heart feels like it's going to beat out of my chest. *I hope that Mason doesn't notice it.*

"What's up, Daddy?" Mason's tiny voice asks.

"So, you know that Auntie Summer and I have known one another for a really long time, right?" Shaw asks as Mason looks up at me, still cuddled into me.

"Yeah, you guys are like brother and sister, but you kiss!" Mason exclaims.

"Well, not really. You see, we're really close, really good friends. And sometimes, friends get closer."

"Okay," Mason says nonchalantly.

"So, I really like Summer. And Summer really likes me," he clears his throat and I see the nervousness in his expression.

I move my arm around Mason and turn him to face me.

"Daddy and I like each other the same way that your mommy and her boyfriend like each other." I say simply, hoping that he understands.

"Are you guys going to get married?" Mason looks between Shaw and me.

"We don't know buddy, but we'll see where it leads," I say.

"Okay," Mason says.

"Okay?" Shaw repeats.

"Yeah. I love Auntie Summer and I love you too, Daddy. It makes sense. It's like caramel and apples. They just go together. Besides, I know Auntie Summer has been sleeping in your room, I saw her that night," Mason snuggles back into me. "Can we still watch Paw Patrol? I want to see if they can rescue Rubble before I have to go to sleep."

Shaw's mouth is open and I'm fighting off laughing.

I guess telling a kid these kinds of things shouldn't be as nerve racking as I was making it up to be. It's not like Mason doesn't know me or like me.

We're family.

TWENTY-THREE

SHAW

MARIE IS STANDING outside my door, but Mason is nowhere to be seen and it's not a drop off day or a planned meeting that I was aware of.

"What's up?" I ask, standing defensively in the doorway.

"We need to talk," she states, her tone dismissive.

Not wanting to be a complete asshole, I open the door and allow her to walk in. She walks through my house slowly, looking around, as if she's never been here before. She's come in a few times when Mason was asleep and she would drop him off. But she's never had any lingering visits and there's been no need for more than a driveway conversation.

I motion to the dinner table and sit across from her with my arms folded over my chest.

"So, what is it?" I ask.

"Did you cheat on me with her?" She asks point blank.

My blood turns to ice and my fists clench, thankfully covered by my arms.

"What?" I ask sternly.

"Summer and you. Did you cheat on me with her?" she repeats.

"I think that you have no ground to stand on here, Marie. You were having a relationship with that guy. My friendship with Summer played no role in what broke us up."

"You still aren't answering my question."

"It doesn't need to be answered because there's no point. Our relationship has been over and done with now for a while. My current relationship status is none of your business."

"How long?" She asks.

"How long what?"

"How long have you been fucking around with Summer?"

"Again, my current relationship status is none of your fucking business. If we aren't talking about Mason, then we do not need to be talking," I stand up and lay both my hands on the table.

"Mason is involved in all of your decisions," she spits back at me.

"You should have thought about that before you cheated on me with Connor. But you weren't, were you?" I seethe.

"Marie, I think you need to leave my house."

"Or what, your little girlfriend is going to come after me?" She sing-songs.

"No, she doesn't need to stoop down to your level. Please get up and leave my house, your accusations are not welcome in my home."

"Accusations? Please. I never trusted you and her together. There was something always strange with your friendship." She shakes her head with a sour look on her face.

"Our friendship was just that, just friends."

"It didn't look that way at the hospital and Mason said that when he was over here that she was sleeping in your bed. I don't want my son exposed to that shit."

"You have no right to dictate who I am with. You hold no capacity of any control in my life. Not now, and not ever. Now, I would like you to leave." I point towards the door.

"You're such a fucking liar, Shaw." she stands and moves around the table towards the front door, opens it and steps on the porch.

From the doorway, I say the last words, "I believe the fucking liar would be you, Marie."

And I slam the door in her face.

My body is tense and I just want to throw something.

How dare she. How dare she insinuate that something happened between Summer and I when she and I were together. When I wasn't the person who broke up the relationship we had. Was I in love with her? I can't really answer that, but I was willing to give it a try. She was having my baby after all, and I was a grown man, well, a young man that was willing to make things work for my child. I never strayed from our relationship when I was with her.

Sure, the crush of Summer had always been in the back of my mind, but I'm a loyal guy and could never bring it upon myself to cheat on someone. I'm sure even if the chick from The Big Bang Theory would approach me for some good times, that my loyalty would still lay with the woman that I am with.

Marie has zero right to accuse me of such things and now my day is ruined. I should never have allowed her into the house. We do not need to have discussions about anything other than Mason.

I slam my fist against the wall and pull back with a stinging on my knuckles. I observe them and thankfully see no blood. I look at the wall and see a small indent and shake my head.

I pull my phone out of my pocket and dial Luke's number.

"Hey bro," he answers.

"Hey, you want to grab a drink?" I ask.

"Um, I've got a meeting in ten, but that should only last an hour, what are you thinking?"

"I'll come to you. I need to get out of the house and I need a deep burn in my throat right now."

"Shit, alright, I'll push the meeting. Meet you in the lobby?"

"Got it."

***

"YOUR DRENCHED, what the fuck dude, did you run here?" Luke asks, holding out his hands in my direction as he approaches.

"I walked here," I state simply.

"Fuck you, you didn't."

"No, I needed to vent out some frustration and walking helped a little."

"Alright, you're going to tell Mr. Luke everything, but first we need some adult nectar in front of us."

"Mr. Luke? That sounds creepy as fuck man, don't call yourself that."

"Do you want to sit on my lap and see what kinds of things pop up?" Luke winks playfully.

"Don't. Don't ever say that to me again."

"What, you afraid of a little man to man action?" Luke wraps his arm around my shoulder and with his other hand squeezes my pec.

"This is all kinds of wrong, let's drink, please? You're creeping me out."

We walk over to the gentlemen's club that is in the back end of the building where Luke works and grab a seat at the bar.

Several business professionals linger around the large brightly lit space in the middle of the day, like coming to this establishment is their job. There look to be a few business meetings happening along the walls in the booths and bigger tables. It's almost something out of the 1950s, where you see Ad Men drinking and spending their evenings before going home to their homemaker wives.

I order a vodka martini and angle my seat towards Luke.

"My ex is a real bitch," I begin. "She's accused me of cheating on her."

"Um, is she aware that one, she cheated on you, and two, that you two have been broken up for quite some damn time?"

I relay the interaction with Marie to Luke and once finished he whistles and shakes his head.

"Dude, I never liked her, she wasn't the friendliest of ghosts."

"I love how I learn after the fact that no one liked her," I roll my eyes and run my thumb along the body of the glass, wiping away condensation.

"I mean, she ran your life. Then she got pregnant and once Mason was born, you were like a glorified babysitter, at least that's how she treated you. You weren't allowed to drive in the car without her, or you always had to have someone else around if she wasn't going to be. I mean, that kind of distrust is disrespectful towards you."

"I know," I agree with him.

"You always have liked Summer though," he points out.

"While that's the truth, I wouldn't have cheated."

"I know that too. You're one faithful old dog."

"Don't refer to me as a dog." I chuckle.

"Woof. I'm a dog too. The chick last night basically yelled that at me when she left my place this morning," Luke shares.

"I don't even want to know," I say shaking my head.

"No, no you don't," he agrees.

And I'm thankful he doesn't dive into his escapades from last night. Most of the time, his stories are some of the grossest stories that I've heard.

TWENTY-FOUR

SHAW

Now that it's my summer break and I have a few weeks off before I need to plan for my summer employment, I place out some feelers to my group of friends for a night out. Summer chimes in immediately that she's ready for whatever I want to do, and I feel thrilled that this is potentially one of the first of many outings that we do as a couple, with our friends around.

One by one, I get notifications from our group that they're in for some mid-week fun and I pull out my laptop and start planning a fun night.

I'm not one to usually be the planner of events, that's generally Summer's area of expertise, but since I've got more time on my hands, I figure that I can take initiative.

I send everyone the address of where to meet for dinner tomorrow night and plan for the rest of our plans to be unveiled there, as a means for no one to really back out.

OUR GROUP IS SEATED along the back wall of an urban pizzeria downtown, one block away from our next destination. The group is a mixture of teachers, business professionals, and couples. We have three couples, if you include Summer and myself and the other five are singles, and not looking.

Summer nor I have made it too known unless you were watching us as closely as Sloane and Luke were about our budding new relationship. We decided yesterday that we didn't want to make a big deal about it, and that we would let it unfold naturally.

"Alright, alright, for us teachers here, this is the time when we get our breaks from the parents that we deal with and sometimes those little monsters. But in the same frame, we miss those little monsters and the constant busy mentality that we have to put up when at work. For you fuckers, who aren't teachers, I hope that each of you get wasted tonight and have to call in sick tomorrow, so cheers to the start of summer. To new love, lots of drinks and a season of good times!" I hold up my beer and everyone else follows.

"So, Shaw, what the hell are we doing tonight and why have you been so tight lipped about it?" Mike, a fellow teacher asks.

"Yeah, we better not be going to a damn strip club!" his girlfriend, Mia mumbles under her breath.

"Hey, when have we ever gone to a strip club as a group?" I ask.

"True, but there was the bachelor party last weekend and it was a strip club crawl," she complained.

"And most of those strip clubs should be condemned. That shit was horrible to watch," Mike rolled his eyes for the benefit of the group, but I saw the small smile on his face saying otherwise.

"Well, guys, tonight I thought we could go and make fools of ourselves," I reply.

"Well, some of us do that without trying. You gotta be a little more concise, my friend," Sloane laughs.

"We're going to the karaoke bar down the street."

"What? I don't sing in public!" Summer says, turning her entire body to face me.

"You didn't even tell your girlfriend?" Luke asks as all heads swivel to Summer and me.

"Wait, what?" Mike's mouth drops open.

"When did this happen?" Our friend Mia asks.

"After you guys all left the BBQ, it was great. I would like to say that I had a hand in finally making it happen," Sloane brushes her shoulders in exaggeration.

"No fucking way? This thing finally happened? It's been what, seven years?"

"Eight, but they're not counting," Luke chimes in.

"You guys, let's get back to talking about this stupid thing that Shaw has planned for us tonight, why?" Summer groans.

"Because it's fun and we've never done it," I smile at her.

"There's a reason behind that," Mike says.

"Yeah, Mike even sounds horrible singing in the shower," Mia replies.

"Gee, thanks babe," he sticks his tongue at her.

"Real grown up there buddy," I say to him. "Look, it will be fun, we'll drink, we'll sing stupid songs and then we'll leave."

"This is the last time you are ever planning anything," someone else from the other end of the table says.

"Seriously, no one should ever have put you in charge. Why did we agree to this?" Tarryn, sitting across from me asks.

"Because we're all lazy," Stephen, sitting beside her replies.

"True, but karaoke? That's the worst kind of thing that you could wish on someone," Tarryn says in return.

"I've decided that I no longer think we should be in a relationship together," Summer says, crossing her arms in a pout.

"Oh babe, you and I are doing a duet."

THE LIGHTS inside the bar are dim and there is an older couple up on the stage singing Sunny and Cher's *I got you, babe.* They're cute, out of tune, but definitely cute.

I pull Summer closer to me and lean into her to whisper, "see it doesn't look so bad."

She side-eyes me and then says something that I cannot hear to Sloane. Likely plotting my death.

We find a few tables and push them together for our group, order some drinks and settle in. At the table, I comb through the song book and then go up to the stage first to add my name and song to the roster. I'll kick off the evening and soon our friends will see how much fun it is and will hopefully follow suit. Singing karaoke has never been something that I've been excited to do, but it's a new venture and I'm always down to do something new.

When my name is called, I stand to the cheers of my friends and grab the microphone and say, "this song goes out to my friends!"

The start of the 'Pour some sugar on me,' by Def Leopard begins and I give my all. In the second chorus, I'm singing and I've missed my step when I'm shaking it up and as I turn, I lose my footing and a loud *oomph* echoes from the microphone as I trip over a speaker at the end of the stage and land on my stomach as the microphone hits me in the eye. The music abruptly stops and Summer runs up to the stage. With her hand placed on my back, she asks if I'm okay.

"My ego is just slightly bruised, but I think that I'm okay. My eye hurts though," I say rolling over onto my back. The emcee steps around me and picks up the microphone.

"Looks like it got too sticky up on stage with all that sugar. Give a hand to Shaw! Up next, we have Saundra!" He offers a hand for me to get up and pulls me to my full height.

"You good man?" he asks escorting me off the stage.

"Yeah, just lost my footing, thanks."

"Come back up when you're ready, that song is always a hit."

I walk back to the group who is cheering and holding up their hands for high-fives. I take my seat beside Summer and she lifts her hand to hold my face, she turns it and takes in my eye.

"I think you're going to have a shiner," she says with a smile.

"Well, that's shitty," I say.

"It's a good story, you got it from karaoke, I mean, who does that?"

"No one. I doubt anyone in history ever has."

"Well, that's a huge accomplishment."

"You have a strange way of looking at things."

I smile at her, because she's sweet in the way she turned around the situation.

When a few of our friends went up to sign up for their turn on stage, I feel like the black eye from my performance is indeed a good story to tell, and the start to a night full of music, drinking and friends.

TWENTY-FIVE

SHAW

I PULL into my driveway and I see an unfamiliar car parked on the curb. As I put my car into park, I see the other car door open and a tall gentleman step out. It takes a moment for me to realize that this is Marie's brother approaching me. I haven't seen him in a few years. He got taller and a lot thinner than the chunky high schooler that I remembered.

"Hey Shaw," he says uncomfortably with his hands in his pockets.

"What's going on, Dean?" I ask cautiously.

"I'm sorry to have to be the one to do this," he says pulling out an envelope from my pocket, taking a step forward and then a step back.

"What's this?" I turn the envelope around in my hand.

"She's taking you back to court, I tried to tell her to take a chill pill, but for some reason she's got this huge stick up her ass and I don't know, man," he shakes his head, then continues. "she's just fuckin' crazy, you know. She's gone ballistic."

"What?" I can't get over the word '*court*'.

"I volunteered to bring this. I wanted you to hear all this from me, and not some idiot that she chose. I know you don't deserve her shit, I know you're a cool guy and a great dad, the whole family does, but you know how she gets, so fucking hot headed and insecure. You shouldn't have to go through this, and I'm sorry."

"But why?" I can't form sentences.

"I think it's because of your friend, or your girlfriend, Summer, isn't that her name? She went on a total rant and made a crap-ton of accusations. None of it was pretty." He shrugs.

"Fuck!" I pound my fist on the back of my car.

"Maybe she won't go through it, maybe she's just blowing steam up your ass."

"No, man. You know her, when she gets something in her mind, it's either do or die. Thanks for being the one to bring this, appreciate it." I say to him as genuinely as I can muster, he doesn't deserve my wrath, she does.

I run my palm over my face, fighting the emotions bubbling in me.

Fuck! I can't believe she has the audacity! What the fuck are her grounds? This is complete bullshit.

"I should get going, I'm sorry Shaw. You don't deserve this shit. Again, man, sorry." Dean holds out his hand towards me.

"Thanks, I wish seeing you was under better circumstances," I offer.

"Me too. Give that little monster a high-five from me, will ya?" Dean walks backwards toward his car as I nod.

I turn around and look up at the house. Summer and Mason are inside, waiting for me to get home so we can have pizza and watch a movie that Mason picked out, and all I want to do is hit something, run away, or just scream.

I ball my fists, straighten my arms and let it fall out of my mouth. The rumbling of frustration spills from my throat. I scream my head off, disrupting the neighborhood and not giving one single fuck. I hear the front door open and hear Mason's scared voice calling my name.

I finally stop my battle cry, look up to the house with Summer and Mason standing in the doorway. Summer's concern is etched across her face as my eyes meet hers. She leans down and whispers something to Mason, who disappears inside the house. I walk up my driveway and once I reach the porch, I lower myself to the bottom step.

Tears erupt from my eyes and Summer pads quickly to me, she wraps her arms around me, and I lay my head on her lap.

"Shhhh. It's going to be okay, Shaw. Everything will be okay." She promises, running her hands through my hair.

"She's taking me back to court," I hold up the envelope that Dean handed to me to Summer.

I haven't looked at the paperwork, I don't want to. If I don't, then I don't know what the details are, and then I won't be heartbroken. Well, more heartbroken.

Summer's hand grips around the envelope and then sets it down beside her as Mason comes outside.

"Is Daddy okay?" he asks.

"Yeah, buddy, he's just sad. Everything will be okay."

Mason runs back inside and a few moments later, I can hear his feet slapping against the hardwood and he returns with his favorite stuffed bunny.

"Here Daddy, Samuel always makes me feel better if I'm sad. You can have him until you feel better." Mason places his stuffed bunny under my chin and then hugs me. I move my arms and keep one wrapped around Summer and wrap my other around Mason.

I take in a deep breath through my nose, close my eyes tight and then let out a shuddering breath.

No one is going to hurt my family.

THE COURT ORDER is Marie asking for full custody and child support.

Currently, our agreement doesn't have child support, as I pointed out the last time she mentioned it, that she would likely have to pay me, because annually she makes more money than I do, by barely anything. I pay my half of everything with Mason, so it's not like I let her pay for everything. The whole co-parenting part of our relationship is almost non-existent unless Marie is pissed off at me. She likes to blame me for things that go wrong on her time and refers to me as the 'fun parent' when I'm anything, but that.

But now, she wants to take everything away from me, and that bullshit is just not going to fly. She has zero grounds for asking for full custody from me. I stay out of trouble, I have a steady job, and own my own home. There is not one black mark on my record which would suggest otherwise.

This whole recent development is simply because she doesn't like that I'm dating someone.

That I'm with Summer.

That I am happy.

Fuck this. Fuck her. She will not take my son away from me.

I SPENT a week finding the perfect lawyer. My previous lawyer moved out of state, and was no longer practicing law here in California, so I asked around and finally landed on someone that was reputable with past clients.

I went back and forth in my emotions and did my best to

reflect that I wasn't internally going insane. Summer often asked how I was and I would smile and nod.

Mediation was next week and I was doing what I could to make sure that my plans for custody was well thought out. I had everything going for me, and she had no grounds to stand on. A mediator would see her claims as bullshit. I was planning to counter her paperwork with a change in my time with Mason, not out of spite, but I figure that I should have equal time with my son. That the relationship ending between us shouldn't fully take me away from my son.

So, at the guidance of my lawyer, I mocked up two plans that I'm hoping will work. Marie won't like this, and I'm not sure if we will be able to work it out in mediation, but I don't see why not?

The morning comes, and I'm pacing the lobby of the courthouse. Summer is sitting on the bench by the water fountain watching me.

"You should sit down," she says softly.

"I need to get the energy out while I can, I don't want to go in there with all this pent up energy, it could be a dangerous situation." I explain.

"I don't think it will make a difference, you're cocked and loaded. Walking back and forth won't change that, take a seat, hold my hand and let me give you enough of my strength to help you."

"You are a true hippy, you know that, right?" I smirk.

"Well, you already knew that getting involved with me," she returns my smirk with one of her own, her dimple peeping out as she tucks a strand of hair behind her ear.

I take a seat beside her, offer her my hand and let her give me whatever good vibes she thinks will transfer to me through our touch.

"You know, this is just a bump in the road, right?" she says bumping her shoulder into mine.

"I do. I'm just pissed that she can be so deceitful and petty."

"You said that she thought you cheated, right?"

"Yeah, she thought that as soon as we got together, albeit years after she and I were together that you and I were secretly seeing one another. I think that's where all this is stemming from. Despite anything that is said to her, she has this crazy idea just from what she saw recently."

Marie and Connor, her boyfriend enter into the lobby, see us, and take a seat on the opposite side of the room. It's almost go time and my nerves are stacked high. My knee is bouncing and I feel a sweat breaking out along my neckline.

The door opens to the mediation room and the mediation lawyer with the firm I hired motions me forward. I approach and shake her hand.

"Mr. Renner, just discuss as what we rehearsed, do not use your anger to fuel conversations and hopefully you will be the winner in the end."

"And if not?" I ask quietly.

"If she doesn't agree with your terms, then you will be working with my colleague on the trial end to fight for your case."

"Right. And so, what you're saying, just so I'm perfectly clear, I know for the millionth time, if we cannot come to an agreement, then court is the next step?"

"You are correct," she states nodding.

"Thank you for your help with this," I hold my hand out to shake hers again. She takes it, nods and goes to sit beside Summer.

TWENTY-SIX

Summer

I FEEL like I've been sitting here on this highly uncomfortable bench for days. Would it be possible that sitting on such a hard surface would mold my ass to a flat surface itself?

I lean to the side, my head hitting the shoulder of the mediation lawyer for Shaw.

"Sorry," I whisper to her.

She's nice, a little straight edge, but pleasant in her demeanor, and she genuinely seems to understand and care about her clients.

"You should get up, move around. I'm sure that it will be awhile before they emerge."

"How long do these things usually last?" I ask standing up, turning to face her and stretching.

"It differs on the complexity of the case and how agreeable both parties are," she offers.

"Great, we'll be here forever." I grumble tightening my pony tail.

I look down to where Marie's boyfriend, Connor is perched on his chair and his head is on his hand, asleep.

Lucky bastard! How is it that men can fall asleep anywhere?

The doors open to the mediation room and I instantly turn around, stand tall and wait for Shaw to emerge. The mediator walks out calmly and then steps aside to let Marie stomp out of the room angrily. Shaw walks out a moment later, shakes hands, says something to the mediator and then walks to me.

I can't tell by the expression on his face, what happened and it's killing me.

He walks into my arms and pushes his head against my neck.

Uncertain of what's happening, I hug him back and wait for him to confide in me.

After a few moments, he pulls away and with a forced smile on his face, he leans in and gently kisses my lips.

He pulls out of my arms and his mediation lawyer stands.

"So, the mediator stated that Marie's requests to gain full custody was ludicrous. Basically, there are no grounds that specify that our arrangement should change based on her requests. However, we will be going to court, because she flipped a lid when I brought up my counter of half time. I proposed a few schedules and well, we'll just say that she didn't like them."

"So, that's great. You won that portion, now it comes to proving the importance of the time split equally. It will be stressful and time consuming, so I would implore that you assure that you're ready and have the support at home." The mediation lawyer says.

I look over to where Marie's boyfriend was sleeping in the chair, they are nowhere to been seen. I can only imagine the anger that she's feeling. Thinking that she had the hand up over ridiculous claims, when the tables got turned.

My gaze returns to Shaw. "So, what's next?" I ask.

"We'll get a court date. I'll set up an appointment to meet with the other lawyer and then showtime," He replies.

He's confident and in a decent mood which is the complete opposite than before he went into that room.

"Let's get out of here," he says holding his hand out to me.

I RECEIVED a text message from Colin, wanting to talk. To give closure to the whole situation, I agreed to meet at a coffee shop close to the book store to make it more convenient for myself.

I sat outside for twenty minutes before he showed up late. He leans in to hug me, but I hold out my hand for him to stop.

"I would rather not," I say quietly for only him to hear.

He nods and takes the seat in front of me, crosses his arms over his chest and leans back. His entire posture is that of an annoyed juvenile, as if him being here is forced upon him. I take a deep breath, lean forward and give him a fake smile.

"Colin, what is it that you wanted to talk about? I need to get back to my shop."

"Oh right. Big business owner and all," he says sarcastically.

I'm happy to be away from that. From someone who thought that my book store was a hobby and not a business. He doesn't appreciate the written word, or for reading. So of course, he wouldn't understand.

"Colin." I say sternly.

"Right, well I haven't seen you and I was wondering what was going on?"

"What's going on? Dude, you cheated on me and I walked in on you with your pants down."

"Yeah, about that. That was a one off," he shrugs off.

"I don't care what that was, you were with another woman. Dick deep. Unprotected dick deep. So, I've been up to getting on with my life without you."

"That's a bit harsh, and I was using protection. I didn't want her to get pregnant or anything."

He's acting like him cheating on me is just a simple task of his day, something that's no big deal. I'm annoyed and really don't want to have any more conversation with him than I really need to.

"Listen, if there's nothing else. I should go," I say placing my hands on the side of the chair and lifting.

"What am I to do with all your stuff?"

"I took what I needed. You can scrap the rest, or give it to your new girlfriend."

"What about the furniture?"

"It's tainted."

"Where are you living now?" He asks.

"Not that it's any of your business, but I'm staying with a friend."

"Shaw come to your rescue? You guys playing house?" he huffs.

"Shut up, Colin."

"What? I'm surprised that it took so long," he sneers suddenly angry.

"What are you talking about?" I clench my jaw.

"Men and women can't be just friends," he states so simply.

I roll my eyes. "Good talking to you, have a nice life, Colin."

I stand up and walk away.

Why did I even bother?

TWENTY-SEVEN

I think if adding this extra layer to us is good, while we may know one another on the friend level, there's a vast amount of other things we save for specific types of relationships. There are still things to learn. Sure, we know what we've seen and when we've been hurt by a relationship, but we don't know about being in that relationship together. We will need to learn how to trust one another in a whole another way—I need to trust Shaw to take care of my heart. And I need to take care of his and Mason's just the same.

I decide that I wanted to do something fun for the three of us. And I think that it would be a nice change from the everyday life we live, especially with court coming soon.

Shaw is sitting on the couch when I come home and turns to me after I close the door.

"What's that look on your face all about?" he asks.

"Let's get away." I say simply sitting beside him on the couch.

"Sure, when?" he agrees easily.

"Wednesday through Saturday," I grin.

"Mason is here," he states.

"I know. Let's involve him. Let's go to Disney." I bounce in my seat.

"Seriously?" he looks at me in confusion.

"Why not? It would be a fun trip. We can space out days between both parks, hang out at the pool at the hotel, all sorts of fun shit."

"That sounds kind of costly." He looks wary.

"Actually, over the years, I've randomly purchased gift cards for just this type of adventure."

"I'm sorry, what?" he looks at me.

"I knew that there would be a time and place to use them." I shrug.

"Well, if you really want to use them with us, then let me grab the hotel rooms. I'll have to let Marie know that we'll be going out of town for a few nights, but okay."

"Why do you have to call her? Isn't it your time with Mason? You should be able to do whatever you want, right?"

"To an extent, it was written in our original custody arrangement when we split up. I only have to let her know that we'll be leaving town for more than a night. It's like a courtesy. It doesn't mean that we won't be able to go, don't worry. Today is Monday, so I'll let her know tomorrow night. Give us a chance to get everything booked and ready." He explains.

"Sounds fair." I smile, "what's for dinner?"

"Takeout?"

After getting our game plan together and reserving everything that was needed, Shaw and I settle in for the night.

A HAND GRAZES the inside of my thigh, lightly trailing from my inner knee up towards my center. I pull in a shaky breath as his fingertips trace my pussy and he gently dips a digit inside, eliciting a small moan from me.

I turn my head and he's staring at me, biting his lower lip as he watches my reactions. I give him a lazy smile, as his finger moves inside me and I open my legs more, allowing him the space.

I arch my neck as he brings me to pleasure.

"Are you just gonna sit there and watch?" I ask in between breaths.

"I want to watch you when you come." He adds another finger and angles his wrist as he pumps, slowly at first until I get used to the additional digit and then moves faster.

"I don't want to come this way. I want to come with you inside me. Please." I beg breathlessly.

"This will be the last time we can be like this for a few days, I want to make this last," he tells me.

"We survived most our lives so far without clawing at each other. I have no doubt that we can look like we're just friends, it wouldn't be anything new."

"Can we have this conversation later, when I'm not trying to have my way with you and make you come on my hand?" he whispers, leaning in and kissing my neck.

I arch my back as he moves his fingers in and out. My fingers are gripping the sheets, I bend my left knee and angle my hips toward him, so he has better access. He withdraws his hand and I hear him mumble something under his breath. He pushes himself up on the bed and hovers over me. He leans his weight on one hand, reaches over me, and into the nightside drawer. With his teeth, he rips open the condom and puts it on.

"I thought you wanted to watch me come?" I grin at him.

"I can watch you come with my cock inside you." He settles in between my legs and a moment later, his hips move forward and he's filling me in the most satisfying way. He pulls back slowly, then thrusts back in. He hisses as I gasp at the fullness. My hands move to his sides to guide his speed. I lift my legs and wrap them around Shaw's lower back.

I was already close when he was fingering me, and the bright lights and weightlessness erupts quickly as he thrusts. I arch my neck, moan loudly, and then squeeze my eyes shut as I feel the excitement pulsing through my body. I feel like I just had an out-of-body experience and when I open my eyes, Shaw is staring down at me with a satisfied smile.

"You are gorgeous." He leans down and captures my lips while his hips continue to move.

SHAW and I have organized everything for the trip and we're both excited to surprise Mason. He's never been to the theme park before, but he's watched all the movies and there's no doubt that this will be fun.

Wow. I planned a trip. Not a girl's trip, or a trip designed for debauchery and craziness. This is a wholesome family trip, something to put the magic in someone else's eyes, and not just my own. Is this what it's like to be a parent? Is that something that I would want, down the road?

I'm excited to see Mason as he runs through the house. While I enjoy the time that Shaw and I get to spend together, it feels like there's something that is missing—just the same. Mason has run down the hallway to his bedroom with his backpack, and a moment later he's running into the kitchen.

"Daddy said that there are some special treats coming?" he exclaims as Shaw has come back inside the house.

He has a smile on his face that screams delight. Comes to stand beside me, leans in and whispers; "That was fun. I'll tell you all about *that* interaction when Mason is distracted." He almost kisses me, but catches himself and pulls away.

"Daddy, where are the special treats? I haven't had any lunch yet, so I could eat whores." Mason grins.

I fight the laughter bubbling from his mispronunciation.

"Horse, it's you are so hungry that you can eat a horse."

"That's what I said," Mason defends.

"Yeah buddy, yeah." Shaw nods. "Well, I'll let Summer tell you about this treat."

Mason looks to me with anticipation.

I pull my phone out of my back pocket and search for a good photo of the park to show him. I go for the patterned flowers at the entrance. That is undeniable. I turn the phone around so he can see the image. It takes a quick moment for him to realize what he's looking at. His eyes light up and his smile grows. He looks up at me, then over to Shaw.

"Are we going... there?" Mason asks.

"We sure are," I say happily.

"Wait, but what are we going to eat?" Mason asks.

As Shaw and I are bringing out stuff to the car, Mason is situated on the couch with his tablet in his hands.

Shaw lingers beside the open trunk that hides us from prying children eyes and reaches for me. Before I can react, his arm wraps around my waist and he pulls me into him.

"I don't think that I can get enough of you," he whispers as his lips gently touch mine.

My hands go around his neck as I kiss him back.

"So, what was it that you were going to tell me?" I ask.

"Oh shit. Yeah, so I told Marie that we would be going out

of town for the rest of the week and she was furious. She blew up. Started saying how she was going to take me to court for wanting to go on a small vacation. I said she was being a hypocrite for all the trips she has taken Mason on this past year. She didn't like to be called out, so that really twisted her buttons even more. I basically had to walk away. She was still yelling when I was walking in the door." He chuckles.

"Ah, so that is what that smile was all about. Oh well, some people see things differently than others. Smart of you to walk away, instead of letting it escalate more. She's the one who looks like a fool for yelling at the house." I tell him.

"Such wise words you have, woman." Shaw kisses my cheek, then pats me on the ass, "we should probably hit the road. I don't think Mason will be able to contain his excitement for too long."

"You're probably right. He's likely ready to burst," I agree.

THE HOTEL IS down the street from the park. With majestic roofs that make it look like a castle and themed art on the walls, Mason is bouncing off the walls.

"Can we go on that one with the flying thing? Can we fly the elephant? Can we go on the train? Will there be super-heroes there? Oh my gosh, can I meet some of them?" Mason asks.

"We can even get their autographs," I tell him, bending down to look at him.

"Are you serious? No fucking way!" he looks between Shaw and me.

"Um, little buddy? We don't say that word, that's a grown-up word." Shaw says with his hand on Mason's shoulder as he lowers to one knee to look Mason in the eyes.

"But mommy says it all the time. Like there was one time, she said it five times in a row." His eyes are wide as he says it. His head swivels between me and his dad.

"Well, mommy is an adult, so she can say things like that." Shaw says slowly, choosing the right words to not bash on his ex.

"When will I be an adult?" Mason asks.

"When you turn 18 and you move out of the house, go to college and live on your own." Shaw explains.

"Oh wow, I get to live on my own?" Mason shrieks in excitement.

Shaw stands and rustles Mason's hair, looks at me, and I return his smile.

"Daddy, can we go swimming?" Mason asks as if the small conversation never happened.

"Sure buddy, go change into your swimsuit." Shaw instructs.

Shaw turns to me once Mason runs into the bathroom.

"Do I swear a lot?" he asks with concern.

"Not too much. Actually, I don't think that you cuss in front of Mason ever." I assure him as he breathes out a hiss of ease.

We watch Mason jump in and out of the pool for a while until it's time for dinner, after a big meal, we get the excited boy into bed and then we crack open the balcony door to sit out there until we go to sleep.

We don't sit out there long and soon we go off to bed as well. We reenter the room and then look at the empty bed parallel to the one that Mason is sleeping in.

"It looks like I get the bed all to myself." I grin, looking at Shaw.

Shaw looks over to Mason in the bed. Sleeping in the middle and completely diagonal with his legs and arms spread. His tiny mouth is wide open and low snores leak out.

"Maybe I can just sleep in that bed with you and sneak out before he wakes up?" Shaw whispers.

"Oh yeah? And what if you don't?" I cross my arms over my chest.

"It's not like we would be doing anything other than sleeping. I can sleep on top of the covers and it will be as if we just fell asleep watching TV," Shaw shrugs.

He has a point.

"Okay, but you can't spoon me." I point my finger at him.

"I don't think that we've ever really spooned, as friends or lovers. In fact, I think there's like a five minute cuddle session and then we will fall asleep without even touching," he replies.

That's true. I can't explain it, it feels like my body can't relax and that it desperately needs to, but someone is touching me, or holding me, or resting on me. I can't deal with it.

"All right, but we'll need the television on to make our story believable." I say.

"You realize he's a kid, right? He's not really going to question what we say." Shaw grins.

"Yeah, yeah, yeah." I roll my eyes.

We jump onto the bed, turn off the beside light and the television. Shaw places his arm under my back and rolls me slightly to face him.

"Now I can make out with you a little before we go to bed," he whispers, closing the distance between us.

I lean up and accept his lips as he slides his tongue into my mouth. My hands slowly roam over the spans of his back. He lightly moans into my mouth when my body presses further into his. I can feel his erection through his shorts and it takes all my control not do anything with it. I feel like we're two teenagers, making out as quietly as possible in a bedroom, while the parents are in the other room. Except this time, I'm making out with someone who is a parent.

TWENTY-EIGHT

Shaw

IT'S BEEN since I was a teenager that I've been to this park. It's still just as cool, even after all the kid rides. Mason's eyes are lit up at everything we pass as he walks in between Summer and I, holding both of our hands. Summer bought him a cool hat with floppy ears and now and then, he will bark like a dog. We decided we would spend the better part of the day at the park and then head back to the hotel for more swimming. Once we ended our day, Mason wasn't even interested in swimming, but decided as soon as we finished dinner, he was going to bed.

So much excitement. Such a little body.

Summer and I have a few drinks out on our balcony for a bit, then we make out a little more before falling asleep.

Another day at the park, filled with excitement, then more back at the hotel pool. We told Mason that he could stay up late and watch a movie with us, but as soon as the movie began, he was out for the night.

It's been hard to keep my interactions friendly with

Summer over the past few days, especially after the kid goes to bed. It's been awhile since I've gone to bed with a massive case of blue balls, let alone for two days in a row. Over the years I've had enough dirty thoughts about Summer to last a lifetime in the spank bank, it's just now that I've had a taste, I want her all the time.

Tonight, I have one hand under her shirt, cupped around her tit when suddenly Mason bolts up into bed. We pull apart so fast that I fall off the bed. Mason didn't see a thing, as he has a vacant look in his eyes, but that jump starts my heart a little. He hasn't asked why Summer and I have slept in the same bed, but then again, he really doesn't seem to care. He knows that we're in a relationship, but I'm not completely sure he knows what that means. Summer has been in his life since day one, and he loves her. He's used to her being around, and even more so now that she lives with us.

A thought that occurred to me when we first told him was that I was scared that he would look at her differently, but he hasn't. In fact, he's always looked to her like she holds a special kind of magic, kind of like I have. They've been thick as thieves since his earliest memory, and I hope that never changes.

Today, we start the day out with breakfast with some characters, and then went back to the park for our last day of fun. We leave the park and head back to the hotel for a quick swim before we drive back home.

Mason is in the backseat watching the scenery as we drive and my hand is nonchalantly on Summer's knee.

"When are you guys going to get married?" Mason asks.

I'm not entirely sure how I don't get into a car accident at that moment as Summer and I both look to one another with wide eyes.

"What makes you ask that, sweetie?" Summer turns her body and looks back at him.

"Because I've known you forever, and I heard mommy say that you guys deserve one another or something," he replies.

"Well buddy, Summer and I haven't talked about stuff like that yet." I say, looking into the rearview mirror to see him.

"Why not? Then I can have two moms." He looks up and meets my eyes in the mirror with a smile.

"We'll figure that out if the time comes. But what do you think about Summer and I being more than friends?"

"It would just be the same with mommy and her boyfriend. One day, Connor will just be another daddy of mine."

I gulp down the horrible thought. I don't want to think of it like that, I'm his only father.

"You just have double the amount of people that love you, little man." Summer grins at him.

Upon getting home from the trip, there's an envelope in the mailbox waiting for me. I look at the sender and notice it's from the courthouse.

I hold my breath as I open the envelope.

I read the contents and see the court date is set and my stomach immediately feels like it's doing somersaults. This is what I wanted. I wanted to get more time with my boy and Marie is fighting everything that I am putting out there. This will be okay. I've got the support of Summer and I know that everything will be okay.

Right?

TWENTY-NINE

"YOU'RE nothing but a total slut, you realize that, don't you? All this time, going after Shaw when he was with me. Weaseling your way in between us, always hanging around. You were sleeping with him, weren't you?" Marie screams from the sidewalk.

I'm standing in front of the bookstore—she pulled her car into a parking space and started walking toward the store twenty minutes ago. I saw her coming and went outside, to not allow her entry or disturb the customers that I have lingering inside. I let one of my staff know to hold the store down and I take whatever she throws at me with my head held high.

I let her yell and say whatever it is that she has to say, without responding. Her accusations are coming at me, one by one. All false.

"And then you whisper shit into his ear about how he needs to take my son away from me, because all you want to do is replace me. I will not let it happen." She points her finger angrily.

I stand my ground, my expression neutral as more insults are hurled at me.

"You know that you're just getting my sloppy seconds. You'll never be the woman that I ever was to him, you know that, right?"

A few onlookers have gathered and are likely now drawing their own conclusions of me being a home wrecker. I still say nothing. There's nothing that I can say to her. She won't listen, she has her mind made up about me.

"Marie!" I hear Shaw from behind her yell.

She turns around in surprise.

"What the hell is going on? Why are you here?" he asks.

"Oh, how nice of you to come to her rescue," Marie sneers.

"Summer has nothing to do with any of the shit between us, and you know it. Why are you causing a scene here?" Shaw asks, coming to stand beside me and crosses his arms over his chest.

"I'm just here to point out all her mistakes." Marie says.

"Summer had nothing to do with our relationship dissolving, and you damn well know it. Now, if you don't leave here now, we will get a restraining order and you bet your ass that won't look good when we go to court." Shaw reaches for my hand and holds on tight in unity.

She says nothing. She looks between the two of us, then down to our joined hands.

Through gritted teeth she takes one step forward and points again, "you both will regret this."

She turns on her heel and stomps back to her car.

Unsure of exactly what she means, I shake my head and then look at Shaw.

"How did you know she was here?" I ask.

"Your staff called me and said there was a confrontation happening in front of the store and that my name was mentioned a lot." He pulls me into him and wraps his arms around me.

"Ah, yeah. I could have handled it on my own, you know." I tell him.

"I have no doubt that you could, but considering we're about to go head-to-head in court, I thought she should know to watch her step."

"Yeah, but you could have used that against her." I tell him.

"I still will, but I don't want to jeopardize her relationship with Mason. I don't want to take him completely away from her. I just want it to be equal."

"I know you do."

"I'm sorry that she came here at you like that. I'm sorry that she's blaming you with these ludicrous things and I'm sorry that you've been pulled into this." Shaw says endearingly.

"You have nothing to apologize for. You have done nothing wrong. You just want what's fair to you." I tell him.

"Thank you for understanding that, but again, I don't want you to be in her firing zone." He tells me as I squeeze my hold on him.

I'M in the kitchen in an empty house listening to a music streaming station of a friend of mine who is a DJ. As I cook dinner for Shaw and myself, my mind drifts back to when I was a little younger and would frequent dance clubs. I move around the kitchen in time with the music, singing some of the words when part of the mix has a song that I know.

"Holy shit! This takes me back to a dance floor with dirt,

underneath the night sky with the morning on the horizon, surrounded by palm trees." Shaw comes into the kitchen.

"I know right, I was going through some of my playlists and remembered that I had everything that this DJ put out."

"Did you date him or something?" Shaw quirks an eyebrow.

"We didn't exactly date, we hung out."

"Oh, I'm sure you did. He's a nice guy if I remember correctly." Shaw taps the counter in the beat with the music.

"Definitely. He's also gotten pretty huge. Last I heard he was traveling all over the place, playing at festivals in other countries."

"You can technically say that you *hung out* with someone who is now famous?" Shaw grins.

"So, dinner tonight, I hope you don't mind, but I'm making Old Bay burgers."

"Are they better burgers than regular burgers?" He cocks his head to the side.

"We'll see how they are. I'm not sure what the hell I'm cooking. It's one of those meal subscription boxes."

"Ah, we're being adventurous in our food, are we?" he jokes.

"You say that now, but once you put my meat in your mouth, you won't be making fun of me then." I quirk an eyebrow.

"Oh, she's got jokes!" he laughs as his phone in his pocket rings. He looks at the caller and answers.

"Hey," he answers. He looks pensive as he listens to the caller, then his eyes dart up to me. "Hold on, let me put you on speaker. Summer is right here." He lays the phone on the counter and a voice comes over the speakerphone.

"Hello?" the voice asks.

"We're both here," Shaw says.

"Good. Okay, so Marie is accusing Summer of harassment."

I cover my mouth in shock.

"That's the opposite of what happened." Shaw said.

"Can you tell me what happened?" the voice asks.

"Well, I was at my bookstore at the front counter, I looked up and saw Marie walking quickly toward my store. I went outside, so she wouldn't disturb my customers."

"What happened next?"

"I let her insult the hell out of me. She practically called me a home wrecker and caused a scene." I explain.

"What did you say?" he asks.

"I just stood there and let her get whatever out of her system. I didn't say one word to her as soon as she started talking."

"What did you say before she started talking?"

"I asked if Mason was okay, but she just started right in on me from there. Other than that I was silent as she went off on me in front of anyone who walked by." I explain.

"And Shaw, were you there as well?"

"No, I received a call from one of Summer's employees. I was close-by and went to her right away," he says.

"What did you say to her at that moment? Nothing that can be incriminating when we're in court?"

"I basically told her that if she continued to confront Summer, that we would get a restraining order and that wouldn't look good for her in court." Shaw says.

"And what did she do from there?"

"She left."

"Have you had any more contact with her since this?"

"No." he and I both say in unison.

"Keep it that way. If you need to speak during drop off and pickups, then do that. Keep it neutral and remember to not talk about any of this with your boy."

"We won't," Shaw says. "With the newest confrontation

with Summer, do you think any of that will make a play in court?" Shaw looks up at me.

"Hopefully not. She may try to use the other day against you in court, but I don't really foresee it becoming an issue. But it might also be wise to have the employee write up an affidavit about what she called you about, just in case we should need it."

"Got it. I'll make sure that it's one of the priorities." Shaw replies.

"Good. I'll be in touch in the next few days. I'm not in front of my schedule, but we will need to work on something to get ready for court at the end of the month."

"Call me whenever you have a chance."

"Will do, you guys have a good night."

THIRTY

Shaw

AFTER THE PHONE call with my lawyer, I feel exhausted and the drama from the custody hearing hasn't even fully unfolded yet. If I'm this exhausted from a single phone call, I can't imagine how Summer is feeling. She's always known how dramatic my ex can be, she's heard and even witnessed some of the events that have unfolded over the years. But now, with her dating me, I'm hoping that none of this will have a negative effect on our relationship.

"The timer will go off in a few minutes, I'm going to run to the bathroom, can you turn it off?" she asks.

I look at her. *Is she okay?* I say nothing, but I nod my head and smile at her.

She's gone for longer than I was expecting. When the timer goes off, I grab the recipe instructions that come with the box and plate our food exactly how it looks in the picture.

When she comes back into the kitchen, I have everything set up on the table, including a bottle of wine.

"Thank you. Sorry, I just needed a breather." She says looking at the table.

"I'm sorry that you've gotten involved with this whole thing and are in the path of Marie's wrath. Let's have a nice night tonight, have whatever this deliciousness is and concentrate on us, yeah?"

"This is Old Bay Burgers, couscous and roasted veggies." She smiles.

We have dinner and it's amazing, I don't hide my satisfaction for it, and I can tell that makes Summer happy. We chat about the day and once we're finished eating, we work side by side to clean up.

"I want to put everything aside. I want to enjoy a night in with my lady." I say, pulling her by the hand to the couch.

"What's on your agenda, mister?" she quirks an eyebrow and grins.

"I was thinking we could finally watch Hamilton and then —" She stops me by throwing her arms around my neck and smothering my face with kisses. I'm walking backwards with her attached to me in her playful attack, dragging her with me as I sit down on the couch.

"You're the best, you're the best, you're the best." She says in between before pulling back. "I thought that you couldn't care less about watching it?"

"Three things. You want to watch it, and I want you to be happy. And of course, I can finally be knowledgeable about some of the one-liners that I hear the kids say in class in the fall."

We settle into the show and I fall asleep before it is over. I'm being nudged awake by Summer when the credits roll.

"So, what did I miss?" I ask.

"See, you already know one of the lines!" She laughs.

Not knowing exactly what she's talking about, I smile, nod and rub my eyes.

"I'm sorry, I don't know why I fell asleep, or how. You were doing a lot of singing. For someone who hasn't seen the show, how do you know all those songs?" I ask.

"Because I've actually watched it before," she says, looking down, then back up at me again.

"Oh really now, how come you didn't say that to me earlier?" I playfully stand up and act like I'm mad.

"Because I would be a fool to deny watching it again." She smiles.

"You're lucky." I point my finger at her.

"Oh, am I?" she crosses her arms over her chest, pushing her tits up in the tank top she's wearing and stands up. She walks over to me and taps her foot, waiting for my response. But instead of something funny to say, I reach for her and grasp her by the neck to pull her against me as I put my back against the wall. My hand travels down from her neck to cup her breast and my mouth takes hers. Her hand moves between us and she cups my dick over my shorts. I press my pelvis into her hand and she rubs me. My hand threads through her hair as I angle her head to kiss her deeply.

"Bedroom." I growl, pulling away from her and grabbing her hand. We hurry down the hall and to my bedroom. I remove my clothes just as she does hers. She moves up on the bed, naked and waiting for me.

I stroke my cock twice as I lick my lips.

"Remind me why we didn't get together until recently?" I ask, crawling up on the bed and between her legs.

"Life just worked out that way," she breathes.

"Well, life is pretty damn good right about now," I reply before my mouth encases her nipple.

I suck, I bite, and I pinch. Her body squirms under my touch as I reach between her legs and feel her wetness. I slide my finger inside her velvety walls and almost lose it right there.

She reaches for the drawer that holds the condoms, grabs one and hands it to me.

"I want you now," she declares.

I don't want to argue or prolong her needs, so I sheathe myself quickly and hold the crown of my cock to her entrance.

Slowly, I push inside her while I relish the feeling of her pussy squeezing my shaft, and as I pull my hips back, I hold my breath. I lean my head back and close my eyes as I move my hips against hers. She meets me thrust for thrust with her hands holding onto my side, digging her nails into my flesh in the best way.

I reach for her breasts and massage them as we make love. She moans, arches her back and bites her lower lip as tiny breaths expel from her. Our bodies are moving against one another, the bedsprings squeaking, and the grunts coming from my throat are the soundtrack to this moment. I never thought that being with Summer in this way was a possibility, and now, I don't want to be anywhere else. She's my endgame, the one that I've been waiting for and I'm the happiest that I've ever been.

We lay in one another's arms with the ceiling fan blowing down on us after my epiphany. She doesn't know that I'm as satisfied as I am. She must think it's because I just came, but it's her. It's always been her.

"I don't want you to take this the wrong way, but thank you." I say.

"Um, you're welcome?" she lightly laughs and turns her head to look at me.

I meet her eyes.

"This isn't just the sex talking, but thank you for choosing me."

"Um, okay." I can tell by her response that she's not sure how to respond, or what I'm really talking about.

"I know that this custody thing is becoming a battle, and

now that you've been caught in some of Marie's crosshairs, I'm sorry about that. But I'm also not, because I have you now. I never thought that anything would happen between us. I never thought that we would be here, in my bed, naked together and not regretting a second of it. We're here together happily and I just can't explain it in any other way than that I love you. I've always loved you."

Her hand reaches up and cups my cheek. She blinks and a tear falls out of the corner.

"I love you too, I do."

I roll over immediately, holding my body over hers, and dip my head to kiss her. My cock is standing at attention again, and in excitement, flexes and bumps against her sensitive skin.

I smile into the kiss, pull back, and look between our bodies.

"I'm never ready this soon," I exclaim, looking back down at her.

THIRTY-ONE

I DON'T WANT to go to work. I want to stay in bed, wrapped around the man who loves me.

We shared that declaration last night, and there was no hesitance in saying it back to him. I've loved Shaw for years as my best friend. And now, we've added this new element to our relationship, being more than friends and everything fits in perfectly. *We* fit in perfectly.

I remove myself from the entanglement of Shaw's legs and walk naked through his room to the bathroom down the hall that all my stuff is in.

I'm at the bookstore an hour later and right away see damage to my storefront. Red paint across the glass, and what looks like some glass on the ground.

I stop in my tracks and look around the area. I turn and look at the parking lot, not seeing anything out of order. There are the standard number of cars normally in the shopping center at opening time, and I don't see anyone lingering or watching, waiting for my reaction.

I pull my phone out of my purse and call the non-emergency police line. Once I'm off the phone with them, I call Shaw, hoping that he would be awake by now.

Shaw arrives moments later, runs up to where I'm standing on the sidewalk.

"Are you okay?" he asks, looking me up and down.

"Yeah, yeah. This was like this when I got here." I tell him.

He wraps me in his embrace, and I lean my cheek against his chest.

"Have you gone inside yet? Is everything okay there?" he questions.

"I haven't moved from this spot. But it looks like there's broken glass on the floor." I push away from him and point to where the storefront looks off. Shaw grabs my hand and squeezes as a cop walks towards us.

"I'm here about a vandalism and a break-in, are you the one who called?" He looks to Shaw.

"No, I called. It's my bookstore. I'm Summer and this is my boyfriend, Shaw."

"Officer Jones. Ma'am, has there been any issues with your store in the past?" he asks.

"No, I've been in this location for six years, never had had any issues." I reply.

"Have you been inside?" he asks.

"Not yet, I didn't want to disrupt a crime scene." I shake my head as another patrol car pulls up. The other police officer walks towards us.

"What do we have here, Jones?"

"Commercial Vandalism and looks like there might also a B & E." Officer Jones replies, pulling out his notepad.

"Here are the keys," I hand the other officer my keys with

the door key out. He takes it and starts walking to the door while Shaw and I stand with Officer Jones.

"Is there anyone that you can think that would do this? Has someone been lingering around the store a lot longer than normal? Have you had any angry customers lately?"

Shaw and I look at one another with raised eyebrows.

"You don't think she would, do you?" I ask.

Shaw shakes his head. "No, she would have too much to lose," he says.

"Who?" Officer Jones asks.

"Well, he's going through a custody thing with his ex. She came here the other day and began yelling all sorts of obscenities at me."

"But she wouldn't do something like this. She knows that she would be at risk of losing custody. She's smarter than that, no matter how dumb she acts." Shaw says, still shaking his head.

The officer takes down Marie's information, and tells us that while it may not be her who did the dirty work, she could still have a played a part in it. After answering a few more general questions, we're waved inside.

All the display cases are on their side, books are scattered everywhere, and posters that were on some of the walls are shredded. Out of caution, the safe didn't have over five hundred dollars in it, and even with it hiding in the floor in the back office, it was found–not broken into.

My point of sale machine is smashed on the floor behind the counter, and my employee iPads are gone. I can't be sure if any books were stolen, but out of everything, that would be the least of my worries.

"What we have appears to be a felony. There is extensive damage to your store that looks to be intentional and not an accident. How many iPads did you have on hand?" the officer asks.

"I had two in the office. They don't seem to be there

anymore. I saw the monitor was shattered as well. But the safe was still intact."

"Insurance will cover the costs of the panes and broken windows. Of course you will have a deductible to pay, but you definitely have a case here. I will reach out with the owners of this center and ask about security footage. Here's my card, call if anything else happens or if you have any additional information. We will also be in touch as information unravels." I shake his hand and turn back to my store.

This is going to take a lot to clean up.

Shaw doesn't leave the store until I leave. I call my insurance, make a claim to have the windows fixed. I catalog what I can of the books, call my employees and Janet, Shaw's mom who is volunteering at the store to give them the time off for a few days while I get the store back in some kind of order. Shaw helps by going to the hardware store and getting plywood to board up the windows. I end my day with a headache and sore muscles.

Shaw had plans to go out to dinner with Luke, which he tried to cancel. I told him to still do his thing, I was going to call Sloane anyway to see if she wanted to come over and I could use a drink.

Slone arrives an hour later with a six-pack of cider and cheeseburgers.

"I feel like I haven't seen you in forever, you get yourself a new boyfriend and suddenly you have no time for your bestie. It's not like schools in session and I can ask Shaw. You can't keep me in the dark. What's going on? Where's lover boy tonight?" Sloane asks.

"Well, Shaw and I are good, our relationship is great, and tonight he's hanging out with Luke." I reply.

"But you look tired," she comments.

"It's been a day, hell it's been a week." I sigh.

"Tell your therapist all about it." She leans back, taking a sip from her bottle.

"God, where would I even begin! So, you know how Marie says that Shaw was cheating on her and all that, well she actually came to the shop and went off on me in front of the store. She was throwing insults left and right, then Shaw came and she left."

"Oh that's fun." Sloane rolls her eyes, "I never once liked her. Sure, I would pretend, but I only did that because the kid is adorable."

I smile, thinking about Mason. "He's a cute kid." I agree with her.

"Okay, so then what?"

"Well, then she accused *me* of harassment. We got a call from Shaw's lawyer last night and I had to run down what happened and what was said. Then Shaw told me that he loved me, and today my store was vandalized."

"Whoa, whoa, whoa! Back up here, Shaw told you he loved you?" Sloane picks her jaw up off the floor.

"Yeah, last night." I nod.

"And?"

"Well, of course I said it back."

"So, you guys are totally in love?" she asks.

"Totally." I say smiling.

"That's lovely. I'm so excited for you. Both of you guys had shitty exes, I'm so glad you took my advice to go after the hot best friend. Okay, so you said something about vandalism, dish."

"Got to the shop today, windows had red paint on them, broken glass, my displays were scattered, and some of the electronics either stolen or busted." I recount.

"Think it was her?"

"No. I think she had something to do it, but she wouldn't directly do it since she is going to court now with Shaw." I reply.

"Even though, she would be an accomplice, right?"

"Something like that. Either way, it's going to look bad if she has any connection. I don't want Mason to be taken away from her, but her jealousy and whatever else is fueling her is going to do some damage."

"Do you think that maybe until all this goes away, you and Shaw should take a step back?"

"No, absolutely not. I don't think that would be helpful. That is exactly what Marie wants. And not by any means something that would be fair to either Shaw or me. She will not win."

"Fair enough. I don't want you guys to do that either. I was just testing you." She grins.

We drink a lot more, and it's not long before my shoulder is being shaken. There are empty bottles on the coffee table and a half-eaten pizza. Sloane is snoring loudly in the recliner, still with a drink in her hand.

"What time is it?" I ask.

"It's just after midnight. Come to bed," he beckons. "I'll get Sloane into the spare room."

Spare room. That's the room that I moved into. I try to not think too deep into his words. I push myself up from the couch and feel like I'm sleepwalking down the hall. I turn into his room, remove my pants and crawl into his bed.

His bed. Our bed. Spare room. My room.

THIRTY-TWO

SHAW

I'VE MET with my lawyer a few times this past week. We've gone over anything that we could possibly be faced with. Summer's storefront has been repaired and the officers haven't been able to link Marie to the crimes. There was video surveillance, but they're having issues linking her to the man in the video. She's been questioned, and while she looked a little fidgety being interrogated, she continues to state that she was innocent.

We had a statement written by Summer's employee who called me, and we are ready for her claim of harassment.

This afternoon is day one of court. I'm not sure what we should expect or how long it all will take, but I'm ready. Summer sits behind me in the courtroom and it's time.

Marie walks in with a sneer on her face. Her boyfriend holding her hand as they walk through the courtroom.

The morning before we went to court, we got a visit from Officer Jones. He had seven photos with him to show us. I looked at each photo but didn't recognize any of the guys. I pulled up her social media and checked her friend's list. None of the guys in the photos were on her friend's list either. We were no closer to finding out who vandalized the bookstore than we were on day one.

There has to be some crumb that was left behind.

The judge asked what kind of custody arrangement that I was seeking. He reviewed the mediator's notes, then asked questions about both Marie and mines financial situations to see if there was capability for me to take on more time with Mason. He also asked how communication was with one another. I was honest. I told the judge about how, despite my attempt to co-parent; we had little communication outside of pickups or drop-offs. Then I told the judge about the confrontation with Summer at her store. The judge looked at Marie with annoyance, who looked at her lawyer with anger. Her lawyer stands up.

"Sir, those accusations are false. His girlfriend harassed my client." The lawyer says with a shaky voice.

My lawyer stands immediately. "Actually, we have a notarized affidavit from a witness about the harassment that took place. It was entered in as item number A4." The bailiff walks over the judge with a piece of paper in a plastic sheet. The judge reviews and then looks at me.

"Is this correct?" he asks.

I nod, "yes, sir." I reply.

The judge then asks about our current arrangement, and what is not working for me. I declared that I wanted more time with my child. As a parent with no negative issues and a good job, I should be granted the same that my ex is granted.

The judge looks at the both of us and stands. "I will have a decision within 30 days for your case. In that time, I would implore you keep your interactions cordial, do not discuss the case with the minor child and to both stay out of trouble."

I stand and shake hands with my lawyer. We both exit and with my hand on the small of Summer's back, we leave the courtroom.

"Easy enough," I sigh, "how do you think it went?" I ask my lawyer.

"I think that the bit about your ex blaming Summer for harassment is a big strike against her. She and her lawyer didn't tell the truth in that moment, and having that signed affidavit was a smart move. That will definitely look favorable for you. Honestly, if you don't get what you're asking for, I would resign from my position. It's a solid case." He replies, holding out his hand to Summer.

She takes his hand and shakes. "Thank you for doing what you do, we appreciate it."

"While you guys don't have the judge's decision yet, go home and celebrate." He looks to the both of us before turning on his heel and walking away.

I look to Summer and pull her closer to me by her waist. I kiss her just below her ear and hear a scoff off to the side, passing us. Not reacting to what I assume is Marie, I continue showing my affection.

"Get a room." I hear a man say.

I laugh against Summer's neck and reach down for her hand. "Let's get out of here, I'm starving."

WE STOPPED at the bookstore on the way home. Summer wanted to check in on her staff and make sure that everything was okay. I feel bad that she's worried about someone coming along again and doing something to her business. I feel especially bad, since we haven't been able to nail down the suspect or tie it to Marie. I know she had something to do with it, and it's only a matter of time before she slips and we get any answers.

The bookstore is packed with customers, so packed that there's a line.

Summer looks elated as she walks inside. My mom, who started volunteering at the store, despite Summer trying to pay her, on the other hand, looks like she could use some help. Summer immediately starts assisting customers who are in line, and in a matter of ten minutes, everyone has been helped. Summer turns to my mom.

"Boy am I glad that you came in here when you did. It's been like that all day," she waves her hand across her face.

"It's been awhile since business has been booming like that." Summer says, looking between us.

"A lot of them said that they heard about the break-in and wanted to show their support. By the way, that new thriller display and the new romance display are empty. I didn't know if you had any more shipment of those, but I haven't had a chance to go check the back room." Mom tells her.

"Thank you for being so amazing, Janet." Summer turns to me. "I'm going to stick around here for a bit, stock up and make sure your mom has some help in case it gets busy again."

"Oh no dear, you guys go along. It's nothing that I can't handle."

"Mom," I say in warning. "I don't want you overdoing it."

"While I may not be a spring chicken anymore, I know how to handle customers. Young man, you remember I used to manage little minds, just like you do. If I could hold down the classroom of thirty wild children, I'm pretty sure that I can handle some voracious readers." She grins.

"Are you sure? I don't want you to handle all the work." Summer puts her hand on my mom's arm.

"Are you kidding me? If I wasn't here, I would sit on the couch doing absolutely nothing. At least here, I'm socializing, I'm moving around and not having my brain melted by television."

I know better than to argue with my mom any further. She's right, she can handle herself.

"Today was the day, right? How did everything go?" Mom looks at me expectantly.

"It went good. I think in our favor and all." I nod.

"When will you know anything?" she asks.

"About a month." I reply, wishing it was immediately.

"Well, I'm sure all will be good. I can't wait to see Mason more. You deserve to see your baby boy as much as possible. You shouldn't be punished just because the relationship with the mother didn't work out."

"Thanks, mom." I reach for her and hug her as she squeezes me tight, I fight back tears.

"Now you two love birds go along and have a good night. If I run into a pickle, I promise to call you."

Two hours later, mom texted.

She ran into a pickle.

THIRTY-THREE

Summer

I RUSH to the bookstore in fear. Along the way to the store Shaw calls the police as soon as his mom texted him with *"There's an angry man here,"*

We arrive at the same time as Officer Jones does.

"Holy shit." Shaw whispers, stopping in his tracks.

"That's his mom is inside," I tell Officer Jones. "She volunteers here."

I see a man in a hood standing in front of Janet and my heart beats out of my chest. I can't see him, or what he's doing, but I can see Janet's terrified eyes. They stay trained on the man in front of her, even as Officer Jones slips into the store.

"I want all the money in the register!" The man yells.

"I'm sorry, I don't have the special code you press to get it to open. I'm new here. I'm just a volunteer." Janet's hands raise in the air as the officer steps into view.

"Put down the gun, son." He growls.

The man's stance tenses and he turns, points the gun in his

hand to Officer Jones and sneers at him. He swivels his head and sees me by the door.

"You. All of this is your fault. You whispered ideas into his head." The man nods his head to Shaw who is standing beside me now, "and now that boy is going to be taken away from his mother." He pierces me with his beady eyes.

"I had nothing to do with what's happening between them."

"Please, she didn't. And that woman behind the counter didn't either." Shaw says, his voice calm.

"Son, I'm going to need you to put down the gun." Officer Jones says.

"She's a home wrecker." The man points at me with his free hand, then looks back to Officer Jones.

"I don't know where you're getting your information, but I'm not. I've always been friends with Shaw, its only recently when it became something more. Please, listen to the officer and put your gun down."

"Please, listen to her. Listen to the officer." Janet pleads.

"I don't believe you." He looks at me.

"I can only tell you my side of the story. I can't speak for what is thought by others. Please, you don't want to do this."

SHAW MEETS Janet and me at the police station. We closed up the bookstore early and followed Officer Jones to the precinct for our statements.

Still not having a clue who the man is, or exactly what his motive was, I'm hoping that Shaw can help provide insight. He doesn't look like any of the men in the photos that were provided, and I don't recognize him.

The mugshot of the man with the gun is brought into the room where the three of us are sitting.

Officer Jones sits in front of us and crosses his arms in front of him.

"He states that your ex doesn't know about what he's done. He is related to her boyfriend, Connor. I believe he is his cousin or something along those lines. He has a pretty dirty record, so these events to your bookstore are not his first run-ins with either B&E's or vandalizing."

"Did he say why he's done it all?" Shaw asks.

"He heard about what has been happening and took it upon himself to take matters into his own hands. He had no endgame, no idea really what he was going to do. It started out with him trying to scare you guys, but it got out of hand as he says. He said that he gained all his knowledge from conversations from his cousin."

"So then he has to know Marie?" Shaw asks.

"He says she's not spoken to him about it. He's been very clear in making sure that it's known that she had nothing to do with his decisions."

"Do you believe him?" I ask Officer Jones.

"I can't be sure. How do you want to handle this?"

"I would like to press charges. He brandished a gun, he stole from me, he defaced my business." I say strongly.

"Very good. Are there any additional actions that you would like to take?" Officer Jones looks to Shaw.

"I would like Connor to come in for questioning, since it's his cousin, I want to hear what he said or did to make these actions happen. And I want to be there." Shaw says.

"We'll make the call. I'll have patrol pick him up tomorrow morning for questioning. I will call you as soon as he's on his way."

"Thank you. If it's all right, my lawyer will be present with me. Since I have an open custody case, I want to make sure that everything is locked and loaded, just in case."

"I'm sorry you guys are having to go through this." Officer Jones closes the file in front of him and stands.

We all stand at the same time.

"Hey, exes be crazy." Janet says and eases up the tension in the room.

THIRTY-FOUR

SHAW

I SIT in the next room watching Connor get questioned. My lawyer is taking notes beside me as I sit there clenching my jaw.

He said that he mentioned everything to his cousins during a night out with them drinking, but he never asked the man to do anything. He said he was angry on behalf of Marie and regrets saying anything to the guys that night. He thought nothing would come out of his complaining, but apparently, he underestimated his cousin. He also mentioned that his girlfriend, my ex, had nothing to do with any of the events that have occurred against Summer's bookstore. We're not completely sure what we can do with that information, but we will provide it to the judge.

Connor made the mistake of using Marie's angry words, and it fueled a protectiveness in one of his family members. My lawyer writes up his report and waits for Officer Jones to provide a copy of the statement to be included in the package to the judge. They assure us that there would be no further escalation of events at the bookstore, as the man was going to be charged and sent to jail with Summer's help.

After all was said and done, I hope that some of the drama would cool down, so Summer and I could enjoy quiet moments without having to look over our shoulders. I feel guilty that she has been impacted as much as she has since we've become more than friends. I owe her a lot of back rubs, foot rubs, or whatever the hell she wants for not throwing in the towel on our relationship, which makes me love her even more.

I intended to show her how much I appreciate her as soon as I return to the house.

Only she beats me to it. I find her laying on her stomach on the bed, wearing only white lace panties. She's reading a book and smiles as I enter the room.

"Can I make a request? I would like this to happen every night." I point to the scene in front of me on the bed.

"It might be something I can arrange." She closes the book and tosses it aside as I approach and then rolls to her back. Her bare breasts are begging for my touch. I palm one breast as I lean down and pull her nipple into my mouth.

She arches into my touch as I strip out of my clothes in tandem with touching her. I move up onto the bed, my hand never losing contact with her body. I pull her panties down and rub my erection against her center as I settle between her open legs. I run my hand across her thigh while my other hand strokes my cock.

"You're my endgame. I don't want to be with anyone else, I don't need to be with anyone else. I love no one else but you and all I can think of right now is feeling you. All of you, in the flesh. I can't remember anyone before you, but if you want me to wait, if you want me to get tested, I will. I just need you to know that I'm dying to fuck you without a condom on." I say to her.

"Since we've started dating, it's only been you too. When I

found out about Colin's cheating, I got tested and I'm clean. If you're wanting to go this next step, then, I'm all in." She tells me.

I push her legs up, so her pussy is bared fully to me. I slide my cock between her pussy lips. Once my cock is fully immersed in her wetness, I slowly enter her. With my hands holding her legs open, I slowly thrust into her. The elation on her face, the sounds of pleasure escaping her soft lips moves me to push faster. Her tits bounce and I move quicker, with her hand moving to her pussy to rub herself as I fuck her. I palm her tit and move, faster and faster, as she massages her pussy. I push in and pull out quickly, slap her pussy and continue. I'm rocking into her, our hips moving against one another as we both move to climax. She cries out in pleasure, her eyes squeezing tight as I piston my hips. Once she comes down from her body high and opens her eyes, I turn her onto her stomach, slap her ass and I pull her hips up. I slap my cock against her pussy again and then push into her, burying myself to the hilt. I take her hips and pull her back and forth on me, my balls slapping against her while I squeeze her hips, she pulses her pussy and I push hard into her and still. I come pulsating in her. I pull back and with the last few drops of my orgasm; I push and pull her pussy along my cock until I can't move anymore.

The feeling of her without the barrier of the condom definitely made me come faster than usual, but I plan to fuck her until the end of our days to build up immunity and fuck her for hours.

And I tell her just that.

EPILOGUE

Shaw

TODAY IS the first day of our new custody agreement.

The judge didn't take kindly to the information on all the damage done to Summer's business and tried to punish Marie for it.

I requested a special meeting between Marie, the Judge and myself when my lawyer told me that rather than 50/50 custody, the judge wanted to flip the arrangements and give Marie less time.

I told the judge, with the guidance of my lawyer, that I didn't want to take time away from Marie. I just wanted it to be equal. I also told the judge that I didn't place any blame from the damage on Marie and that I didn't think she should pay for others' sins.

Marie was shocked. The judge was shocked.

I just wanted to see my boy as much as she did. I got what I wanted.

Despite the distrust and dislike that I hold for Marie, I asked her that we explain the new arrangement to Mason together in a neutral setting. So, we met at Denny's, and explained everything to him. Mason being the awesome kid that he is, just wanted reassurance that neither of us were going anywhere and that he was safe.

He was. And he will forever be. He's got enough people in his corner to make that happen. Despite my ill feelings towards Connor and the role he unknowingly played against Summer, he's been a figure in Mason's life just the same.

There is nothing I wouldn't do for my boy, and I think the fact that I fought for him proves that.

With Mason and I in the car, I want to make a quick stop before going home. I pull my car into a parking spot and turn around to him.

"Hey buddy, you remember when we were in the car coming back from Disney a few weeks ago? You asked me a question."

"About Summer becoming my other mommy for real instead of my auntie?" he says without even thinking about it.

"Yes, about that. Would that be something that would be okay with you?" I ask him.

"I think it would be cool."

I tell him what we're doing and he's just about as excited as I am when we walk inside and browse the glass cases. Mason helps me pick out something that is modest and not too flashy, and as we walk inside the house, my pocket instantly feels like it's weighted down.

I have no actual plan. I just want to put my ring on her finger with the promise that my best friend will be forever mine.

Mason runs into the house before me and rushes up to Summer with a hug.

"Hey buddy, I missed you." Summer ruffles his hair.

"Hey Summer, my daddy has something for you." Mason points at me as I'm closing the front door.

Well, it looks like there's no time to prepare.

Summer looks to me expectantly. "Oh yeah? What's up? Did you bring home something good for dinner tonight?" She looks around, sees no bags and looks confused.

"I thought that maybe the three of us could go out to dinner. You know as a celebration of a sort." Knowing that she will think that I'm talking about the new custody changes.

"Oh, I think that's a great idea." She smiles.

"Yeah, we can celebrate all the good things." Mason claps.

THANKFULLY, Mason doesn't press on for me to give Summer the ring the rest of the day and he doesn't give it away to her either. I make reservations at a nice steak restaurant and we all get dressed up to head out to dinner. We walk into the restaurant and I pull out the chair for Summer, then make sure that Mason is seated properly as well.

The maître-de hands us the menus, then asks; "are we here celebrating anything special tonight, a birthday perhaps?"

Just as I say, 'not really,' Mason perks up and says loudly: "Daddy is going to ask a special question."

Summer immediately darts her eyes to me in surprise.

I hide my face with my hands and shake my head.

"Well, crap," I stand up, push my hand inside my jacket pocket and move to one knee. Summer turns to the side, facing me.

"Since Mason can't keep his trap shut," I hold out the ring box to her. Mason immediately gets up and stands beside me.

Before I can even speak, "Auntie Summer, will you become my other mommy?" he jumps up and down.

I have no words. The kid took them away from me and with a hopeful glance up at Summer, she has her hands over her mouth, tears in her eyes and she's looking straight at Mason nodding in acceptance.

THE END

ACKNOWLEDGMENTS

I wrote this book off of a drunken conversation with my husband after a signing. He wanted me to write a book about a typical dad. And so, that's what I did. I sat on this novella for awhile, thinking that I wouldn't write it. But here I am... bringing it to the readers for some feel good, heartwarming friends to lovers goodness. I hope you enjoyed it.

So thank you, Mr. Anders for giving me the idea.

Thank you, the readers number one for reading!

Thank you to my tribe, Jess, Maren, & Mary for in one way or another supporting me.

JUST THANK YOU.

DEAR FRIENDS,

Thank you so much for your support. If you enjoyed this book, please sign up for my newsletters so you can be in the know when a new book comes out, or if you just want to hear me ramble about nonsense.

My newsletter has sneak peeks of upcoming books, give-aways, and also fun stuff. SIGN UP HERE

Please check out my website at: WWW. TARRAHANDERS.COM

I hope that in some shape or form you felt connected to my characters, I strive to have my stories be as relatable as possible, and not too outrageous. The sole purpose for me to bring my friends these stories is to feel like that too can be you.

That being said, I write to make you happy. I wouldn't be able to do so without your feedback. Whether if you leave a review on your favorite book retail site (Please do that would be spectacular) or if you feel like shooting me a message at: tarrah.anders@gmail.com . I would love to hear from you.

All my best,
Smooches ~ Tarrah

xoxo

Tarrah Anders

The Melted Series

Do you want more info about Tarrah Anders and her releases? Sign up for her VIP Newsletter today!